DANCING LEDGE

A wild and windy rain soaked night on the Dorset coast -
South of England. February in the Millennium Year 2000.
Severe weather warnings are in force, gusting to gale
force nine, all along the coastline of Dorset.

A rain battered Land Rover driven by young Ian Samways
from the garage of Swingle Matravers, with several other
members of the village careers along a steep rutted pot
holed track, perilously close to the cliff edge. The sea
crashing black and boiling against the rocks far below. The
Land Rover fighting to avoid disaster from sliding over the
edge in the dark.

A night of severe weather warnings put out by the BBC
for the whole of the South and West coast of England.
Four people already lost to the elements according to news
broadcasts. All during the past three days and nights.
People who had ignored the weather warnings and thought
they knew better. The emergency services on the alert for
more whilst the hurricane storm lasted. The "Robert
Charles Brown" Mersey class lifeboat of Swanage already
having been called out twice from Swanage during the
week to rescue yachtsman in distress.
The Land Rover is heading towards a ship: the Phoebe - a
rust bucket of a tramp steamer built just after the 2nd World
War and now marooned by gigantic waves on the rocks at
Dancing Ledge, a rocky promontory jutting out to sea.
Dancing Ledge had hidden cross currants and underwater
obstructions that most people in boats or small ships would

not go near in daytime, let alone at midnight with barely a quarter moon to light there way along the cliff edge road. Especially as the Coastguard lookout post at the promontory known as Peveril Point above Swanage, was only now manned during the daytime by volunteers - and certainly not during the small hours of the night.

CHAPTER ONE.   The PHOEBE.

Fred Driver, pig farmer and chairman of the Swingle Matravers 'Committee for Wealth' shouting above the din from the back of the Land Rover as it plunged on with Ian Samways at the wheel: 'Anybody know anything about this ship - the Phoebe or whatever she is?
'Christ Ian! watch where your going you idiot - you almost had us over !   - this from Bill Hutchings the chemist.
'Your not sports testing some old biddies car you know, after giving it one short your MOT's - this is dangerous!' .
Hanging on as he said this to an improvised rope strap on his side of the back seat. Trying not to look out the door at the sea boiling far below.

'Very funny!' Said Ian, who was in fact very careful when servicing other peoples cars. Especially old ladies. One of them might go and have a word with one of his older relatives after all! And there were plenty of them living in Swingle Matravers.   Wresting the wheel violently to avoid yet another gaping hole in the path come track that ran along above the cliffs. Headlights probing forward in the pitch darkness. Rain - like stair rods - coming down continuously. Windscreen wipers creaking asthmatically as they tried to clear the murk and muck off the screen.

Ancient wipers leaving streaks of dirt across the glass in the process. Not helping visibility.

As mentioned Ian could be meticulous in dealing with other peoples vehicles during servicing. He cared little for his own battered pick up truck or Land Rover. Both were lucky if they got an oil change or indeed their tires pumped up properly once a year.

 'I'm trying to get there before the coastguard!!   You saw the maroons (rockets) go up at Swanage!? Two of them -- meaning "Coastguard Rescue".   There'll be on their way along that road - about 20 minutes by my reckoning....'
The coastguard were based at the back of the former terraced coastguard houses at Peveril Point over the other side of Swanage pier. One Maroon going up meant the Coastguard only would attend in their Land Rover. Two Maroon's meant the Lifeboat - inshore semi rigid inflatable or large lifeboat to attend. Three Maroon's meant both the coastguard and lifeboat.

'I feel sick' - this from Linda Dodswell.
'You could always take one of your Aromatherapy tonics Linda, might do you more good than it does when you rub it in on the tourists! This again from Bill Hutchings the local chemist. Bill, a tall, silver haired gentlemanly looking man in his mid sixties with a telling sense of humour. When he had a mind to use it that is. Not the sort of person you would expect to be in on this sort of caper. But

there again you could never take anybody at face value in Swingle Matravers. Foolish to do so.
'I don't find that very funny Bill! Said Linda. Anyway there not for consuming by mouth. Their massage oils remember!'   Linda retches and just stops herself from being sick. 'I might also remind you that you sell my oils in your shop. For which you get a commission - 25% !

'Aye your right' said Bill. ' It's not much' Linda retches again. Bill continues: ' This woman comes in the other day, wanted something for her headaches.   I sold her your: " Lemon Seaweed Laxative drink". Cured her headaches all right. No prizes for guessing where she spent most of her time over the next 24 hours!...
She wants a refund and *he* is talking of complaining to Trading Standards.!   You can understand their feelings....!
Linda: 'She's not getting any' - meaning the money.
'No' said Bill. And neither is he!!   'I do feel sick' said Linda.

Ian calls out about it being another twenty minutes or a bit less. A large tree looms into view across the grassy track. 'Watch it for Christs sake' shouts Fred. 'Sorry! Blown down by the look of it'
 'Brilliant deduction Holmes!'.

Fred: 'Stop winging Ian'.   'You asked if you could drive remember...'
Ian, 'Only because its my Land Rover'.

'Don't you trust us then?' came another voice from the back.

'Lights!!' In the distance through the rain two car headlights can be dimly seen. 'The Coastguard!' yelled Fred 'That's all we need. The ruddy Coastguard turning up!'.

Linda. 'Told you we'd get caught!' Ian. 'No it's alright - they've turned off up towards the lighthouse - over to Durlstone'.

Bill 'Lets hope they stay there - we're almost up to the wreck!'
Bill again 'How the hell can we bloody well get on board the Phoebe if the Coastguard are hanging about!? The others look at him in astonishment of the language heard from such a carefully spoken man.

Ian: ' The Victorians did this sort of thing – and so can we! Then: 'We're here!'
At the top of the cliff they can see the ominous black shape of the ship, prow down, moving from side to side, groaning like a trapped beast. A deep rocky crevice in the ledge holding the ship in its vice.

Linda : Is this a good thing or what? Nobody answers.
Fred: 'You all agreed' we're here now. After all I *am* the Chairman of the 'Committee for Wealth!'.

Bill: ' We all *know* you're the blasted Chairman Fred!'.
'It's because of that we're here!'.

They climb out and Ian goes round the back to gets a rope
ladder out of the back and stands there unfolding it.
Ian: 'The Ledge is about eighty feet down and far too long
for this thing; but we can get down the grass slope about
twenty feet down. We scramble down the rocks from there
but we'll have to be damn careful. A lot of it's fallen away
with coastal erosion - and the rocks will be as wet as
anything'.

Linda: Can't we just go down the way the tourists do?
Further along where the steps are?
Fred, speaking low and gesturing with a flattening gesture
of his palms for the rest to do the same : 'No. That's where
the Coastguard will be. See?' Pointing.
Linda: I can't see anything in all this wind and rain!
Ssshh......! from the others.

Bill: ' We need to get down the other side. The ship will
hide us from them. Where we can't be seen in all this
muck! You can rely on the coastguard being near the steps
- this is a wreck remember - you get dodgy people trying
to get on board - and it's a danger to shipping'. Shades of
that film "Whiskey Galore" thought Linda, but she said
nothing.   The irony of what Bill is saying is lost on the
group in the howling wind and rain.
No point in antagonizing the men Linda thought to herself.
She was going to be staying on top to act as lookout, with

a torch to warn the raiding party below. All those second world war films this lot watch, she thought.   Look at them! All wearing ex army camouflage jackets from the army surplus in Wareham, with beany hats and wellington boots. Honestly what do they look like!

Ian threw the ladder down. Snaking away in the blackness. The moon parted and they could just about see the end of the rope resting on what was left of the grassy slope twenty feet below. The rocky scree disappearing into the darkness.   Fred turning back to the Land Rover gave a start: 'Kill the lights Ian for Gods sake! Don't want to make things that easy for the Coastguard do we?!' Sheepishly Ian runs back over to the Land Rover and does so.

Linda goes and sits huddled in the drivers seat of the Land Rover to keep a lookout. The others start the perilous descent to the dark hulk of the ship grinding and moving on the ledge below.

Very slowly, hand over hand, with the sound of stones being dislodged and bits of stone falling on their heads they make their individual way down the rope ladder. At last huddled in the lee of the wind behind a protruding boulder, they flash their pen torches to try and see the boulder strewn slope that leads down at a steep angle.

'What the Hell are we doing this for' grumbled Bill to himself.   'Come on, no use waiting here freezing to death.

Coastguard will be up to us soon' said Fred, ignoring Bill's comment.

They start to make there way Indian file down the slope, keeping away from the darker area to the left -- thin air where the grass has fallen away.
'Watch it!' cried Ian, its gone completely here! They cling on and move round a great gaping chasm in the ground. No one speaks. But all with the same thought. Is the 'Committee for Wealth of Swingle Matravers' really worth all this? And for what? Seeing what they can pinch off an old tub like this. All those stories of smuggling on the Dorset coast. That's why we're here. Trying to pretend we are all part of a great Dorset tradition of Smuggling. Tilly Whim caves where smugglers we're supposed to go to hide from the patrols in the 1800s! They say that smuggling still goes on at Mevagissey in Cornwall....
These and other thoughts stew around their collectives brains as they make their perilous descent to the black hole for shipping that Dancing Ledge had become, and the even blacker ominous bulk of a ship stranded on the rocks.. The prow looming up high above them as they reached the wet, sea washed ledge. The rain lashed ship creaking and groaning.
 'How do we get up that!?' said Hillery Jenkin, farm labourer and general

dogsbody on Fred's pig and cattle farm. More used to handling animals and tractors than situations like this. But he had proved useful in the past on other exploits. No

room in Ian's Land Rover for him. He'd got to Dancing
Ledge by walking overland from Worth Matravers.
Keeping an eye out for the Coastguard as he dodged from
field to field down to the Ledge itself.   Lanky and rough
hewn, he was the ideal type for this sort of venture..
People had learnt not to laugh at his name "Hillery". If he
landed a punch it was doubtful you would get up without
the aid of a first aider.

'We get up there with this! said Fred. 'Now watch'. 'Saw
one of these used in that film "When Eight Bells Toll".
Producing a rocket fired grappling hook from his rucksack.
'Army surplus' said Fred, in answer to the varied
comments.
They all huddle back behind rocks as Fred fires the rocket
grapple up at the top of the ships railing. The attached
rope and vicious looking three pronged hook flying
upwards and wrapping itself around a railing at the prow
of the ship. A second explosive hook is launched and
similarly wraps itself around a stanchion just above the
hawse hole for the anchor chain not far from the first.

A torch suddenly starts flashing urgently from above.
Three short and one long - repeated continuously, until
Fred, taking his torch gives one short acknowledgement,
keeping certain to be round the other side of the ship away
from the steps leading up to the western side of the ledge
where the coastguard would be approaching. They'd
probably heard the sound of the explosive charge when the
hook was shot off.

'Damn!' said Fred, recognizing the recall signal Linda was giving. 'Means the coastguard are on the move. We'll have to be quick'.
They start climbing the thin rope snaking down out of the gloom from the top of the ship. Bracing their legs on the ships side. Hillery grunting encouragement to Bill further up who is not used to all this. Also by far the oldest in the group. In the distance on the other side of Dancing Ledge, pinpricks of light about half a mile off as vehicles can be seen making their way over the rocky headland towards the ledge. They would have been delayed because of the cliff falls that had gone on.. Dancing Ledge was more or less out of bounds to the public and others due to dangerous cliff. The Committee had thought that they would have time to negotiate such hazards. But they had not allowed for a recent change of management in the Coastguard. A new person had taken over, recently retired from the Army and all vim and go. No one on the Committee for Wealth knew his name yet, but the coastguard who, contrary to cynical local opinion, we're not all semi retired part timers and volunteers, had been galvanized into a much more active role by the newcomer.

Fred, Bill, John, Ian and Hillery all stood on the deck getting their breath, gasping and coughing at the effort to get up here. People more used to looking at animals or standing behind shop counters. Now staring at the rusted upper cabin deck. The black eyeless windows of the bridge staring back. Bits of tackle and deck furniture rolling loose with the ships every movement. Threatening to trip an unwary visitor in the pitch dark. The whole upper deck shuddering with the impact of the waves. The ship leaning at a steep angle. Rusted deck rivets popping and banging as the hulk that was once a seagoing vessel starts to give way.

'No time to lose' shouted Fred and he dished out instructions as to who should go where. Telling them all not to go below the main cabin decks where the black boiling sea is now moving dangerously through the ship. They moved carefully forward, fearful of the ships sudden lurching from side to side. Canvas sacks in hand to carry what they could salvage. The light starts flashing again from the cliff top. 'Linda's doing the emergency signal again!, said Fred. Muttered oafs and expletives as they fan out in the almost pitch dark, trying not to fall over stanchions and who knew what rolling around in the gangways. Sometimes lit by the half moon and then in complete darkness as the ship rolled. They fan out. Fred and Bill to the Bridge and Captains cabin cum chart room. The others moving along in and out of the half dozen cabins which the sea water had not yet reached. The Phoebe had been licensed to take passengers, the cabins behind the Bridge structure being for that purpose. Crew quarters we're down below. But no one was going down there! The thought of corpses of the drowned floating around in the lower decks, was more than most of them could stomach. The captain and the deck crew, those who had been in the deck cabins we're known to have got off. But by no means all the people on board had been so lucky down on the mess decks lower down. The Phoebe had been carrying extra crew for security but no one knew why and the captain, a man nearing his retirement and now recovering in hospital was keeping his mouth shut. Aided and abetted by some secretive people who had come visiting both he and the ships first and second mates when they had just been admitted almost a week ago now. All in all just six people had got off the ship. But another five we're still missing. And that was just the regular complement and not the security extras that the survivors, questioned by the police, did not seem to know about.

On the Phoebe the Swingle Matravers 'smugglers', aware of seconds rather than minutes left to them we're frantically going in and out of cabins grabbing anything they could. Cigarettes, loose fixtures and fittings, money, watches, jewellery and clothing. Anything not needed being donated to the Seamans Mission in Poole where the survivors we're billeted

.

In the Captains cabin behind the Bridge deck Bill Hutchings is rummaging through anything he can find. Not much here but there is a brown paper package of a triangular oblong shape. Wrapped up in waterproof greaseproof paper by the look of it, and with a very secure outer canvas bag. He does not see the small blue and red lights winking on and off inside the package. The canvas bag is the sort used for dropping overboard in an emergency. The whole thing is weighted down with what feels like lead shot. No time to find out now what is in it.

Bill hoists the heavy bag up with its long rough loop of cord for carrying over the shoulder and throwing in to the sea if it has to be slung overboard.

Up on the bridge Fred is going from locker to locker. The Bridge house with its conning wheel and instruments grouped together around the voice pipe to the engine room. The equipment looked old except for the radio equipment which was shiny and obviously recent.   Quite out of place compared to all the other rudimentary ships equipment that looks as though it dates back to the early 1950s. Likewise there was a ships radar which still had its cover over it. The cover like the equipment looked brand new and completely out of place on such a rust bucket as this ship - tramp steamer - undoubtably was. The radar had obviously not been in use and no doubt the reason why the Phoebe had founded in such bad weather.   The crusty old Greek captain, such we're his origins, preferring to use his own knowledge and skills rather than rely on newfangled electronic equipment recently installed by the ships owners.   Likewise the radio telephone looked as though it had not had much use either. Fred, who in a former life before marriage and pig farming had gone to sea in the Merchant Service as a ships radio operator, stood for a moment admiring the equipment. He'd not been in the officer class but had been a leading seaman in the radio rooms of Merchant ships working the shipping routes to the far East the Congolese and Ivory coast. Moving goods and general merchandise exported between England and the far East. General carriers the Jupiter Line had been. Fred musing on all this eyed up the radio equipment and regretted not having the time to unscrew it all and get it ashore. The shiny black Marconi radio telephone looked particularly good. He sighed and moved on. Maybe he could come back later...? Or perhaps not.. The ships creaking and swaying telling him that time was fast running out.

Fred had been regarded as very good at his job in the Merchant Service . Joining in the late 1960s and doing the job, after training in Southampton for a good ten years. Fred's two older brothers and sister had all married and settled down away from the family farm. Fred after leaving school had attended an old fashioned local college to do an HND in Business Studies. But the tutors had not been up to much and the College, a hotch potch of decrepit drafty buildings and even more decrepit looking teachers, had proved sadly uninspiring for a young man of Fred's tender years. He'd left for the Merchant Service after a year of a two year course. His parents had not objected. They'd invited two of the colleges' tutors round to their house for tea when their youngest son had been a couple of months into the course. The two threadbare stooping characters with their long academic faces who'd turned up on their doorstep had not impressed either parent, and had succumbed to the very detailed questioning Fred's Father had subjected them to about the occupational value of the course allied to future employment prospects after leaving college. Fred's father was not known for his patients with strangers and the tutors had been virtually booted out of the house half way through their tea! Fred had gone off into the Merchant Service with his parents blessing and had not looked back. The Jupiter Line based in Southampton and with agents in every port of significance around the world had fast modern mixed load ships and up to date equipment.

Starting as a deck hand and with plenty of training opportunities within the Shipping Line consisting of some twelve large cargo ships plying routes to the far East and the Americas, Fred had quickly developed a surprising aptitude for signals and telegraph work. Passing all his technical exams and becoming a leading hand in the radio room. Travelling all over the world. Eventually leaving with a good service record and enhanced pay off for good conduct. And the gratitude of the shipping line.

Fred returning to England, marrying a local girl, Jane he had been corresponding with and seeing during his leave taking. Settling down to take over his fathers pig farm which was in something of a sorry state due to his parents failing health and lack of investment. Other members of the family taking no interest in it at all apart from spending odd days helping out when their parents health had taken a turn for the worst and one or both of them had been in hospital.

Fred had spent the next eight years building it all up, concentrating on pig farming in particular. Though cows also took a part in the farm life as well. But it was pigs that he and his wife concentrated on. Moving into the farm

building a separate Annex to live in and looking after
Fred's parents at the same time. . But all too late to save
his parents health sadly. Fred had been able to obtain the
services of an outreach nurse who came to the farm, plus
other home care help for which he had to pay privately.
Neither parent had wanted to go into the local care homes
available.   Both we're now buried in the Swingle
Matravers church yard under a handsome gravestone. A
bench seat nearby under a mayflower tree, with white and
pink flowers (his mothers favourite type), with a plaque
paying further tribute to their lives.

Back on the Phoebe the situation was getting worse. The
weather was bad, waves crashed over the forecastle of the
ship, which groaned and lurched from side to side. Each
movement frightening to see when near to the darkened
ship looming above. The alarm signal. Light from
Linda's torch flashing continuously from the cliff top.
Canvas bags containing cabin loot tied to a long line and
passed quickly down the side of the ship to waiting hands
below. The bags being released, the line hauled back up.
Bags passed hand over hand to the base of the cliff where
another line snaked up to where Linda stands at the top,
hauling bag up the rocky slope. Throwing the line down
for the next one to be attached.   Hillery now scrambling
up the steep slope to give Linda a hand at the top.
Fred with a last look at the Phoebe, hastily climbing down
the rope with Ian behind. Both keeping a watchful eye out.
Neither of them needing to tell the other to get a move on.
The ships nightmarish shifts from one side to the other

getting more pronounced as the ship tries to work herself free from the deep rock crevice her bows are stuck fast in. But not for long by the look of it.

At the base of the cliff swift progress was made up the grass slope to a point roughly half way up, and then the rope ladder up to the top. Passing Hillery still checking on the rope to make sure the last of the bags didn't snag. The group involved in too many mid night nefarious activities to worry about this escapade.

But what had happened to the coastguard Land Rover? They should have been here ages ago?! Mysteriously they had held off. Surely they would have seen Linda's flashing torch light and the answering light from Fred? The moon was not good but surely they would have been spotted in the half moonlight on the deck of Phoebe? Unbeknown to the amateur smugglers there had, in fact, been a further landslip in the bad weather. Part of the cliff over towards St Aldhelms head where the two coastguard Land Rovers we're coming from had given way. The coastguard being forced to reverse; calling up the emergency services to block off the lanes from Worth Matravers towards the cliffs to stop any curious passer by getting too close. Even on a night like this there would be ghoulish people out and about. Inquisitive visitors from camp sites and the rest. The coastguard would be distracted further by the need to keep visitors safe. Those who lived near the Headland over to Winsprit and Winsprit Bottom. West Man and St Aldhelms head itself.

Determining to find out later what people we're doing on the Phoebe. For now that would have to wait.
A lucky break for the Swingle group but, as they we're to find out later they we're *not* off the hook as far as the coastguard we're concerned!

Meanwhile the remaining party from the Phoebe led by Fred Driver having scrambled up the grass slope had regained the Land Rover and started throwing all the bags full of pickings from the ship into the grilled off area at the back. Suddenly a terrific grinding noise below. Running to the edge and staring down they saw the Phoebe, unable to withstand the pounding she'd been getting sliding stern first nearer to the edge of the Ledge.... The villagers needed no second bidding. A sudden crash of forked lighting revealed the other side of the inlet. An enormous cliff fall that had stopped the coastguard from coming closer. Horrendous. Seeming to move back further away and towards St Aldhelms head, where the coastguard had first been spotted. Or rather there bright headlights which we're familiar to the villagers.

'Get in and let's get going' said Fred impatiently . Enough of all this for one night'. Ian started the engine and turned the Land Rover heading back up the slope of the field towards the track above. The wind behind them now, pushing the Land Rover from behind. Ian hanging on to the steering wheel peering through the windscreen. Wipers going against the rain as it slanted thickly across the windscreen. Slewing the Land Rover inland and away from the Ledge - now fast disappearing into the darkness and leaving the nightmare of the Phoebe behind. No one said anything. They just preyed the Land Rover would not tip over. Almost too soon.   Suddenly s yawning black hole where the track should have been. 'Christ!!' shouted Ian swinging the wheel violently to the left and sending the Land Rover vehicle crashing through a National Trust fence and into another field away from what had been the track. Gunning the engine and moving further inland. Grunts and cries from the back as people we're thrown about. Luckily the new set of wide deep treaded tires bit into the weld of the ground. The vehicle rocking from side to side as it made its way up the curving slope of the field. The Land Rover. Its engine loud in its efforts. The rain still lashing down. Occasional thunder. Suddenly a flash of lightning making everybody jump.

The National Trust had been working on the ground at the top of the field, putting down a short stone road up the steepest part of the track before the top . A dry stone wall loomed up. Ian turned the Land Rover, following a bridal path along to the gate fastened only with the metal hook and eye so common in these parts of the cliff area. The Lower, Middle and Upper paths leading from Durlston country park over towards Langton and Worth Matravers. Farm fence gates. Ian got out, ordering the rest to stay put. They needed no second bidding. Swinging the gate open they repeated the manoeuvre until the tramp steamer raiding party, cramped in the back of the Land Rover, finally bumped onto the open road that led to Worth

Matravers and beyond to Swingle, and sanctuary at the Drunken Cow where Stewart the landlord would be waiting in the narrow darkened entrance at the back to let them in through a door normally kept locked.

It was now past One O'clock in the morning, going on for Two. The Swingle Matravers contingent are moving fast along the back lanes towards the pub. Keeping a wary eye out for police and coastguard patrols.

CHAPTER TWO.
THE PUB AND THE CUSTOMS AND EXCISE.

The pub was in darkness when they arrived. The last of the regulars having gone through the back door an hour earlier. Only Jane Driver, Fred's wife remained talking to Stewart. She had come earlier to check up on what was happening. None of the regulars remarking on why Jane was staying behind when they eventually left. Nobody talked in Swingle. Or at least very little.

Ian drove quietly round the back of the pub. Not wanting to attract attention. The rain had left off and just a gusty wind blew nothing more harmful than leaves across the car park. A weak moon showed fitfully through scudding clouds.

 A dim emergency light showed at a side door. Stewart the landlord stood in the darkness. The lights completely out in the car park and only dimmed lights on and those at the very back of the pub. Hardly any showing through the curtained doorway. The Swingle Matravers Committee for Wealth had arrived. They moved about silently.

Unloading the canvas bags from the back of the Land Rover. Forming a chain to manhandle the bags into the back of the Drunken Cow and the little used further back parlour next to the kitchen area; normally kept locked as there we're better furnished rooms at the front for the passing trade to sup and eat their pasty and chips. These latter supplied a coterie of ladies from the village. Cooked up in their houses and brought to the pub daily to be warmed up in the microwave before being put into the display units. The pub providing employment for quite a few of the locals in this way. In the summer walking tours we're organized from the pub, meals and accommodation thrown in. But this was winter now. And what was going on in the back of the pub at this ungodly hour was not for any tourists eyes or ears. There we're none staying at the pub now. The No Vacancies sign hung, clearly visible from the road. Hooked on under the pubs now famous large sign of a cow leaning in a drunk and contented manner against a fence, straw in its mouth and a galvanized trough full of the local brew at its feet. "Swingle Ales get them going" picked out in faded black and gold lettering along the bottom of the sign. Creaking loudly too and fro in the wind.

The back rooms side lights we're now on. The Land Rover and the pubs back door now both securely locked. Thick damask curtains hung over any space where the light might show from outside. The landlord Stewart being well used to this type of smuggling operation. His own family had been involved in the smuggling trade for over a hundred years, or so Stewart liked to give out to the tourists all looking for that authentic bit of Dorset that they could record and take home... Stewart hinting at Cornish smuggling connections around Mevagissey, one of the principal haunts of smuggling in the West Country of England, and had been so for centuries. Still so today if the stories we're to be even half believed.

In truth Stewart had seen on TV and read the tie up book published of Poldark. Had visited Charlestown, St Austell where they had done a lot of location filming. Did not want to shatter any illusions the visitor might have now...

Soon all the smugglers bags from the Phoebe we're in the room from the corridor beyond. At least nine or ten of them covering several tables.. The group we're settling down to whiskies and beers and in Linda's case Sherry. Getting warm by the log fire banked up in the grate. But not so much that the smoke and cinders going up the chimney be suspicious to passers by - so late at night. The locals we're not so much the problem. They might be out shooting rabbits or the like and in any case we're more likely to keep their mouth shut in case their own nefarious 'doings' came to light. But you never knew where the police, and especially the customs or coastguard might be snooping around. They we're less easy to 'nobble' as far as Stewart was concerned. Stewart and his family lived above the pub at the back. Any chimney making smoke would be put down to them. It was well known that the Drunken Cow had seen little modernization since it had been built in the very late 1950s. That, as Stewart and his wife and three children would say, most certainly included the cramped and damp married quarters accommodation provided on the top floor at the back under the very roof eves of the pub. A nasty set of rooms with the wind whistling around the bare bricks of the chimney stack. I'll fitting windows, much filled in with decorators mastic, old newspapers and large strips of cellophane sellotaped on. The latter to act as secondary glazing. A polite way to describe it!

Luckily both he and Joan we're very capable of making do with what they we're served up with. Being much experienced in the vagaries of pub management. The Drunken Cow had been through at least two owners since Stewart and his wife had moved in five years ago. Developing their spurious local history about being a smuggling family. The truth being a lot more cosmopolitan. Luckily to the pubs current owners, a property company based in Singapore, the Drunken Cow was just one very small entry at the end of a long list of similar catering and hotel properties the world over. Managed at arms length by London agents who restricted themselves to sending a six monthly profit return to the owners.
Nevertheless the pub was a welcome sight to those who had been through the traumatic events of the evening. Plates of steak and ale kept warm on the kitchen hot plate had been consumed. Pints and other drinks dispensed. Clothing changed to get people warm again. At last with

the clock approaching 2am Jane looked at her husband:
'Well can we begin then?   'Just a mo missus' said Fred
downing his pint, the third since he had sat down.
Ahhhh..! Rubbing his stomach with satisfaction. Right
let's get this lot sorted'.

Soon there was just the sound of bags being emptied and
the scratching of pens as the contents we're logged and put
into piles.   A weird assortment it was too.: Cigarettes,
matches, old fishermans clothing, maps of the coastline
and ports of entry, telescope and compass and assorted bric
a brac. All from the shelves on the bridge wheel house and
the cabins further aft. There came assorted clothing,
personal effects from side lockers, a truss, portable radios
and money left lying about. For an hour there is silence.
Sorting through, categorizing, discarding where necessary
to give back to the Phoebe's captain and crew, those that
had survived, being looked after at the Sailors Home in
Poole. Left round the back of that fiercely white painted
building with its large: ' Sailors Rest' sign painted in blue
along the front. Receiving whatever help and support the
social services deemed fit to dole out.

The lists we're just being finished and the effects about to
be discussed when there was a loud thumping and banging
from the other side of the main pub doorway.
'Coastguard!! Open up!' came a shout through the thick
wood.
Complete panic. Everybody throwing the piles of bric a
brac and clothing into sacks. The trap door hidden under

the carpet pulled up and the sacks thrown down in a
disused cellar and the carpet. The settle pulled back over it.
Linda and Hillery sitting on it and looking as though they
we're having a last drink before going home to their
respective haunts.

Stewart nods at Fred and they both go across towards the
sounds of Mr Holmroyd the senior customs officer on duty
that night, still bawling through the door. Now grudgingly
pulled open by Stewart who peers out bleary eyed as
though he has been in bed and hastily dressed to open the
door.

Mr Holmroyd, a big man striding into the room. ' Good
Evening Stewart! Would like to have a little chat with you
if you don't mind. Oh! What a surprise Fred's here.
About a ship that I believe he was taking a remarkable
interest in a few hours earlier. In the middle of the night!'
'Me' ?! Said Fred. Shuffling off looking like an old man
and wearing bewildered look on this face. 'Aye You! Mr
Driver - in a Land Rover down at the Ledge. Like the one
parked at the back. One of your little escapades is it'?

'What little escapade would that be Mr Holmroyd?, Only
went out for a ride...
'Rubbish! ., at gone midnight?!'
 My lads saw you down by the Phoebe before it slid off
that ledge into deep water! They swear they saw you and a
group of others boarding the wreck earlier. Hardly miss it
with all the torch flashing and that exploding gun thing

you had for shooting grapnels up onto the ship! Really!
What we're you trying to do, compete with the thunder and
lighting. Hear that sharp crack of the explosion for miles!
Foolhardy escapade in my opinion at any time, and in this
weather?!

Linda Dodswell walked out from the back area wearing a
dirty pinny rubbing her arms and hands on a dish cloth and
looking for all the world as though she had been clearing
up in the kitchen all evening on a late shift at the pub.
'We we're just deciding on whether to go home' says
Linda.   Holmroyd stares hard at her, saying nothing.
Brushes past her into the back area by the kitchen.
He runs straight into the others: Bill Hutchins, John
Hobson and Ian Samways with Hillery Jenkins. Also Jane
Driver. All trying to look as though they had been playing
cards and forgotten the time. Empty glasses at their side.
Trying to make it look as though they we're just finishing
their hand before going home and had forgotten the time.

 Mr Holmroyd: 'Very cosy. Your up late aren't you? Not
been out along the coast tonight'? This with heavy handed
sarcasm.
 They just look at him blank faced and carry on...
Jane, Fred's wife attempting small talk - as the coastguard
had never entered the pub: 'Best be packing up I reckon.
Vicar we're here earlier and said we ought not to be
drinking so late after hours'.
Holmroyd: ' The Vicar!? From what I've heard of him
I'm surprised he's not here with you! And before waiting

for a reply from any of the seated individuals: 'Best be getting home then hadn't you!? - as Miss Dodswell was saying'.

As they get up to leave, Holmroyd, walking off towards the main door shouts back his parting shot: 'Think I'm fooled don't you! We'll I'm not. I'll be keeping an eye on you lot from now on... And if any odd looking stuff turns up in the flea markets around here or Dorchester or anywhere else I'll know where to come looking!' With that he stamps out followed by his two much younger colleagues. The others sit silently looking at each other and at the closed door of the pub...

The Tramp - Gentlemen of the road.

Out on the road a tramp lying in a ditch by a hedge drunk . Old clothes, filthy hair and clutching a carrier bag, inside of which is a black bag, and inside that a brown paper parcel which emits a soft hum. Two tiny lights, red and blue in colour are winking on and off.

Stinking for want of a bath the tramp is singing a bawdy song: ' Show me the way to go home!   I'm tired and I wanna go to bed....' Followed by: 'Rosy Rosy where are you, where are you now...'

The group meanwhile have left the pub, agreeing when to meet again on the morrow. Making their separate ways home. Linda Dodswell, collected her car from the

Drunken Cow car park and is driving the short distance to the edge of Swingle and her cottage, when in the darkness she sees a shape and recognises it.   Winds down the window.

'Henry isn't it ? .

Henry. ' Don't call me that, don't call me that!'.

Linda soothingly: ' Alright Henry I won't call you that' Now what's that you've got there Henry?   Seeing the bag or bags within each other.

Henry 'It's mine, mine!' 'Of course it is of course it is' says Linda as though soothing a child. 'I just wondered what it was that's all'.

Henry: Lay off me! Leave me alone!'.

Linda: I'm only trying to help Henry - tell me what's in the bag?

Henry: ' A man dropped it from the sky.

Linda: 'Don't be silly Henry. Tell me what happened . What is it then....? (Still in her soothing cooing voice).

Henry: 'No!'.

Linda reaches out of the car window trying to get the bag. 'Come along Henry let's just look at the bag.

Henry: 'Leave it!'.

Linda: adopting a much firmer tone.   'Now Henry, if you don't show me I'm to have to call the Police - you know that'.

 Henry maundering on to himself about the police and how they treat vagrants. What their police cells are like. Muttering about life.

Linda takes the bag from him quietly and looks inside. A dark shiny rectangular object, quite heavy. Some electric

gizmo with small red and blue flashing lights going on and off continuously. Also in the bag is what looks like a mains lead with a booklet in French. Instructions with pen pictures relating to a row of controls, evidently concealed underneath a plastic lid that is held down with tiny screws.
Linda: 'Now Henry I'm going to take you in my car to the Salvation Army Hostel in Swanage. You can have a good nights rest, and a bath and a shave. Yes and a hot meal as well.
Henry reluctantly heaving himself into the car . Linda seeing his bulk, tactfully leaving the window wide open. The stench is almost overpowering.
Making sure the package is on the back seat away from Henry's eyes. Out of sight out of mind she hopes.
Linda guns the little engine of her car and they speed towards Swanage and the all night Salvation Army hostel and the night staff on duty there. At least they know Henry and he knows them... Hopefully the bathroom will be free.....and the disinfectant....

CHAPTER THREE.
THE DEVICE.   JOHN HOBSON'S BUTCHERS SHOP.

The following Monday morning at the back of John Hobson's Butchers shop. Linda Dodswell, has called by with the bag wrested from Henry the Tramp. Taken out of its wrappings he and Linda are standing staring at a black canvas bag containing a triangular metal box or device that appears to have buttons and switches on it. Two tiny lights, the size of pin pricks appear to be flashing on and off. The front of the box has, what looks like African writing. Though it is scratched and not very clear and looks as though it was put on later and someone has been hastily trying to clean it off.   There is what looks like an instruction manual. A damp damaged looking booklet of about twelve pages and measuring some 10 inches by 8 inches, and fastened in a black plastic ring binder. Appears to be written in French. A reference on the front, in very small lettering to the Credit Lyons Bank in Paris, France.

'I've a bad feeling about all this' said John looking down doubtfully at this device that is now sat on the butchers slab winking away with its two tiny lights. 'Think its some sort of explosive?'. Can you hear any ticking?
 'From a Bank!? Don't be daft!' Said Linda .
John looked mulish: 'It could be!'. Turning the bag over and over in his hand. So far none of them had told the police or anybody else, apart that is from Fred Driver as the head of the Committee for Wealth. John keeps nervously fidgeting with the wrappings and trying to make sense of the booklet. 'It's heavy you know this device...'
Linda: ' For goodness sake. Stop playing with the bloody thing and give it to me!'   This said in tones that her therapy patients rarely heard.
She drops the bag on the table. A lid on the side of the device is dislodged. More flashing lights. Red and blue on the surface of the casing, green and yellow lights inside a recessed area containing the controls. Linda backing away behind one of the big fridges: 'It's a bomb!'

'I don't think so' came John's now reassuring tone. He
picks it up and looks more closely at the bag. The buzzing
noise and other sounds from the fridges in the kitchen not
helping. The fridges contain carcasses of sheep, and parts
of cows to be cut up later. The room is very cold.
John: ' Come out of there you daft..... hiding behind that
thing. Then: ' The back of the lid has some instructions on
it in French <u>and</u> English by the look of it... think your
meant to connect it up to a computer that has stockbroker
Share prices on it. Something about software to be used to
download the forecasts it makes.
We need to get Fred round here. He'll know what to do .
John: 'Fred Driver?! - all he knows is pigs!'
Linda importantly: 'He's the Chairman of the Committee
for Wealth of Swingle Matravers. He was also a Leading
Radio Operator in the Merchant Service. He knew Radar
as well. He took exams. Different levels. Or have you
forgotten?! Of all of us he's the one with the technical
knowledge to make sense of this! Then muttering: 'We
could sell it - whatever it is to the highest bidder'.

'I know I know' said John tiredly. Belatedly recollecting
his customers at the front of the shop. Going off to deal
with them, including the curious, standing around
wondering what on earth is happening that is so important
to keep the butcher away from his customers.. Linda now
making some tea with the electric kettle. Finding the
biscuits. Clearing the kitchen table at the side of the
butchers slab in the middle of the back room. Switching on

the electric heater to give some warmth in this, essentially,
refrigerated area.

A knock on the back door and the tall elegant silver haired
visage of Bill Hutchings, mid 60s, the village Chemist
smiles through the tiny side window before entering the
back door. Looking very different now to the blacked up
image of a would be smuggler going on board the Phoebe
only 24 hours earlier.   Looking, not surprisingly hung
over with about three hours sleep. Coming round for a
quiet mid morning chat with his friend John and surprised
to see Linda now also transformed back into the village
Aromatherapist bustling about the kitchen. Bill is wearing
his white chemist's dispensing coat, smartly creased down
the sleeves. Black lace up shoes polished bright and
shining. Bill was a man noted for maintaining standards,
no matter what the situation. He kept silver haired tabby
cats which he exhibited and which regularly beat the
competition, be it local or further afield. Exhibiting in the
large Regional Competitions that we're held twice a year
in London and Manchester. Though essentially a
Pharmacist by Profession he had a keen amateur interest in
Silver Tabby cats. The kittens they occasionally produced
we're in high demand. Coming as they did with all the
registered paperwork and the required inoculations.   There
we're no flies on Bill as the saying goes. Or on the cats for
that matter! Linda tells him about the device and the fact
that they are waiting for Fred and anybody else on the
Committee who might turn up. This so as to decide next
steps. Bill goes through and nods to John who at that

moment is selling some nourishing meat to one of the older residents of Swingle. Actually the leftovers from cow and pig that usually went into the waste bins if the butcher could not shift it off the counter any other way. Whether the oldies who came in realised what it actually was, was another matter. The smell from the pig bins at the back was appalling.

A sound of tires on gravel and a long black shiny expensive car coming into the yard. Fred Driver had arrived. Goldie an elderly arthritic Retriever with dark golden hair and watery eyes lies sprawled across the opposite seat. Fred, although a hard nosed businessman whereas pigs we're concerned, was very sentimental indeed about dogs and cats. Rather too susceptible, some would say to a hard luck story from the local rescue centre, if the truth be told.
The appeal to Fred's soft nature where pets we're concerned had worked, and now Goldie wondered stiff legged along behind her new master Fred, fascinated by all the new smells around the farm buildings that now abounded her daily waking life. Probably realizing that she had found a safe billet at last after all those months watching strange people (the Social Services) coming and going to see her then owner, one Albert Grout. Grout, an odd job man all his life had lived in a damp terraced house in a back street area in the north east part of Swingle where the water ran off the low hillside that abounded that part of the village and where the more hardened type youth lived. Large squalling families. Junk yard front gardens.

Very old council housing stock representing the cheapest and worst kind. All kept well away from the touristy high street with its very old buildings that people came to see and photograph. Grout had been a heavy smoker all his life and now paying for it with his health. The coughing and spitting had grown worse and his wife of eighteen years marriage had finally left him for more conducive surroundings. Oxygen cylinders and a face mask with an outreach nurse visiting. At least the council had cleared up the front garden and cleaners had more recently been round the inside of the house with maintenance men stripping and repairing the walls where the worst of the damp came in. They'd drawn a line at one of their own staff having to visit such a place. In truth the area was scheduled for demolition but there'd been trouble rehousing the people who lived there. Word had spread as to what they we're like, and having "problem families" moving in on your doorstep was not everyone's cup of tea.

Goldie had spent hours lying on a piece of old carpet on the drafty floor by his owners bed; trying to be a comfort. Wet nose stuck on top of the blankets. Looking dolefully at his master lying there inert . "Good dog, good dog....". Or following his master as he tottered around the flower beds or vegetable patch. Once it had been Mr Grout's wife that would follow him around in case he fell over. Mrs Grout had, unsurprisingly, suffered from a lot of chest complaints caused by the damp. Forever 'down the doctors' as the neighbours called it, getting treatment. Eventually things had taken a turn for the worse. Too late she had been admitted to hospital. By some miracle recovering sufficiently to be able to move out into a warden aided council bed sitter where she could better be kept an eye on. A local charity helping provide her with furniture and collecting her belongings and providing her with some new clothes. The old ones hanging in the wardrobe at her former marital home not being worth saving. Though she had insisted on some of them which had been thorough washed and cleaned.

Now it was just the dog at the terraced house to keep Mr Grout company. Or had been before Mr Grout had almost forcibly been stuck, protesting as he went, into a council run nursing home. Social Services fed up with endlessly calling round to see him. At least they had made sure the dog was alright. One of their number being acquainted with Pig Farmer's wife Jane and hearing that he was partial to domestic animals and the dog, looking particularly pathetic when they had both called at the re homing centre, had found a new place to stay.

Fred looking slightly askance at the dog which was now spread across the leather seating of his very expensive vintage Rolls Royce Silver Cloud, that his long stint of a pig and cattle farmer had finally allowed him to buy. Previously used for Weddings but the owner had gone bankrupt and had sold it at a much reduced price for cash. Something Fred had a considerable amount of stashed away in various places. Better than the bank he reckoned. Pity he'd forgotten to put the rug on the seat! Hairs all over the place... Jane, his wife was not going to be pleased when she next got out of the car in Wareham high street and discovered dog hairs all over the back of her dress. Queening it down the high street to the *Penelope and Claribella* Tea Rooms; only for her to notice too late, the rather obvious effect that the dog had had on her coat as she had got out of the car. Much to the cynical amusement of her so called 'friends' greeting her on the pavement outside the entrance. Also not helped by Fred smelling of pig and insisting on helping her out of the car using old world courtesy that she normally appreciated. Fred coming across the yard and getting into his magnificent shiny Rolls Royce, kept clean by a mobile cleaning company, without bothering to change anything more than his wellington boots.   Though the car could be said to be a substantial step up from the thirty year old slurry wagon inherited from his father that he'd used for years on end to give his wife a lift into town.   Both Fred himself and his father before him. Some of the slurry slopping out of the back of the truck as Jane clambered down from the high instep on her side of the truck. On one memorable occasion right slap bang in the middle of genteel Bournemouth! The truck lurching to a halt on the slope leading to the pedestrianized entrance of the famous Burlington Arcade. Giving the well to do matrons of Bournemouth a right load of farmers ozone when emerging and carrying their shopping bags from: Beales, Debenhams or Marks and Spencer . Fred as usual, forgetting to put the tarpaulin covers over the open back of the pick up truck; resulting in a thick mat of flies getting everywhere as he drove past.

Meanwhile back at the Butchers shop Fred leaving the dog fast asleep and with a window wide open for ventilation, walked into the back of the hygienically butchers shop with all the usual farm aromas wafting about. Linda, noticing the pungent aroma slipping behind him with the air freshener. Keeping the back door ajar as well.

Fred nods a greeting to Linda and Bill who are sitting around the kitchen table drinking tea and looking through newspapers. The back of the shop was a throw back. Formica table with four chairs. Electric kettle on the side and an old Tricity Contessa cooker from the 1970s and still going strong. Though the cooker switch was now useless and one of the struts to the upper lid at the front concealing the grill, had gone. A modern microwave stood nearby. Lino on the floor. In truth the kitchen area was a memory to John's late wife and he could not bear to part with any of it. But he kept all that to himself.

The window at the back looking out into the shared parking space for John's butchers shop, plus the florist next door, then Patel's grocers followed by Neal's newsagents. Much further over could be seen separate parking for the local Jobcentre with its fire door exit at the back. The staff currently taking their fag breaks out the back on the concrete slabs that made up the back entrance.

'Morning Fred' said Bill getting up and eying the vintage Silver Cloud Rolls Royce parked up at the back and now blocking in at least two other cars of more common appearance. Hopefully neither the newsagent or the florist we're going to want to use either of their cars during the next half hour or so! Just then John comes through from the front, at last having been able to put up the: "Back in ten minutes" sign.

'Your car!' said Bill admiringly. 'Wish my overdraft would pay for one like that, not earning enough from my chemist shop to do more than pay for my living and that of my two part time assistants. Fred ignores the comment, having heard it all a dozen times before. Lot of nonsense where Bill Hutching's was concerned.

John ' Making a lot of money from Pigs Fred? ' Fred: ' Not much - what about your butchers shop'. 'Not much' John replies. 'Nough said' said Fred.
'Where you'd plan to go on holiday then Fred?' said Linda, not wanting to be left out. 'Missus wanted to go to Australia' said Fred. 'And you booked it? Said Bill. 'Nah..! We booked Barbados instead. 'Five star hotel was it?' said Linda. 'Matter of fact it is'. –

 'We've booked New Zealand' said Bill not wanting to be outdone. The "we" in this case being Bill's latest girlfriend, one of a succession he'd had since his wife had died some twelve years earlier. Bill in his 60s still good looking to women. Tall, silver haired and slim build and known to have a solid bank balance. A natural draw to women in the middle of their lives and just lost a partner of their own. Looking round for a likely prospect. Sometimes for the second or third time running...

The others however stare at him. Bill was a frugal man. His normal stamping ground for holidays was a fortnight in Corfu, or 8 nights in Rome on a Co-oP package deal. Saving his money for his holiday property investments. These comprised a part share in a string of caravan sites from Exmouth to Weymouth. Plus a part shareholder portfolio investment with others, in a string of pubs on the Isle of Wight. All organised into an investment group by a retired Finance Adviser who lived over to Wimborne. Bill did not talk about his money outside local 'Committee for Wealth' village concerns that is. Even at that he restricted himself to nodding wisely at the meetings it held and making mild suggestions.

Fred put his mug down with a thump. 'Right let's get a look at it then. Not got long, middle of the day you know for the farm. Lot to do...'
John Hobson hands the package over to Fred. So saying they all settle down, mugs of tea at their elbows. Absently sipping at them and nibbling at biscuits whilst leaning forward to watch Fred do his work with a small wallet of fine tipped screwdrivers, pliers and a large old piece of testing equipment in a battered suitcase that he'd dragged in from the car. Meanwhile developments we're occurring elsewhere...

CHAPTER FOUR.
THE EMBASSY OF BHARUN, LONDON.

The Bharunian Embassy, a three stored tenement building
was located in the Whitechapel, Aldgate East area of
London where Jack the Ripper was said to have done some
of his best work. Where most people would be careful
even today to walk in broad daylight, let alone at night.
The gloomy Victorian tiled underground tube station of
Aldgate East, waiting for either a District or Hammersmith
and City line train, was not a place to be on a deserted
Sunday night for example. Standing at the end of the
platform and looking back at the stairs from the entrance
waiting to see if the feet and legs of the person who had
been following you through the dark foggy streets we're
going to appear coming down the steps. Aware as you
stood watching and waiting, that there we're no station
staff around to assist you, and the tube train was not for
another 18 minutes.

The Bharunian Embassy boosted a large over ornate office
with red curtains and thick carpets full of African furniture
not all of what could be described as original. Dominated
by a huge gaudy chair fashioned in a parody of a throne,
with massive arms and back. The whole edifice featuring a
garish display of coloured beads, strips of gold and bright
red cloth tacked onto the wood in wild profusion. Walls
of the room covered with African spears and shields,

though how much of it had ever seen an actual African village, or indeed the people inhabiting such a village that a western culture imagined that it consisted of, was a very moot point. Bought wholesale as a job lot off a market stall? Some young couple getting rid of a load of junk left over from clearing out a relatives house? Somebody, perhaps, who had spent most of his or her retirement buying tourist tat from package holidays to Eastern Europe, Africa and the Middle East. Who knew!? They looked impressive at any rate, or so Prince Okamba thought..

Prince Okamba the 35 year old African son and one of the numerous members of the Bharunian ruling class now sat on this Embassy 'throne' and proceeding to tell everybody how the secret stock market, gathered to hear from their leader as to how the forecasting device came to be lost in Dorset in the first place. He is staring at the culprit - Embassy driver Mr Lupie Shalmin..

Prince Okamba is dressed in flowing African robes created by one of his six wives who all live in cramped quarters at the top of the Embassy. These being all of his wives he had been able to accommodate without getting too many complaints from the locals not used to the ways of foreign embassies.

'So', said Prince Okamba, staring accusingly at the Embassy driver standing nervously in front of him and the assembled staff of the Embassy. ' You all know why we are here this morning'. A fawning silence greets this announcement. Nobody is going to interrupt this nutter from the palace in Oshasha. Okamba taking, it was rumoured, so many pills each morning that he was regarded by many as a walking junkie. Prince Okamba points dramatically at the thin man, balding, in his early thirties and wearing a thin ill fitting jacket and trousers. The Embassy Driver. Now standing on the thick piled carpet and quaking in real fear. He has already been roughed up by the Embassy heavies in the basement; on the orders of Okamba himself.

'We are here - he thunders - to discuss the stupidity of Lupie Shalmin who, when he was down on the Dorset coast on a *personal* errand for me last week. Lost a most valuable piece of Embassy Equipment. Which, despite *knowing* that it was valuable he left lying about on the back seat of his car! '

Lupie: ' Please please! - it was not my fault. It was late at night and I was tired and trying to find my overnight board and lodging. I had driven all the way down from Whitechapel, I was tired and stopped by the roadside to try and find out what the rattling noise was in the boot of the car. How was I to know that a tramp was there in the ditch when I got out. Suddenly there was this big smell, I turned round in the dark, no street lamps, and this old man was running off with it.......

'How dare you interrupt me! Standing up and pointing
with his cane at the driver. 'I who am Ambassador to this
Country on behalf of His Majesty King Obanda the 3rd of
Bharun, a much revered cousin'.
The driver quakes in his shoes and tries to shrink into the
carpet.
Prince Okamba sits back in his chair and growls: 'I will
deal with the driver later', flicking out his ornate cane,
like the tongue of a snake, at the driver. Satisfied with the
affect he has had upon the poor unfortunate.
' Let us now turn to the question of the recovery from the
British villagers of this most valuable object. Sulu Wasei -
our Head of Intelligence will now speak.

Sulu Wasei is a sleek young man just turned 30. By
backward Bharunian standards he is well educated and not
without a sense of humour - when he gets the opportunity
to display it. Which with Okamba, the weirdo from
Oshasha, is not very often.

Sulu moves over and right away from Prince Okamba's
desk and over elaborate chair. This move in order to
emphasize his own stature, and of course to distance
himself from other influences.

'My extensive researches over the past twenty four hours
have led to an acute understanding of that area of Dorset,
England. – I visited the public library in Tooting - South
London'. Laughter from some of the audience.

Prince Okamba: 'That's enough! Have you no respect for your Head of Intelligence who has only recently come amongst us from our glorious capital Oshasha?'   More sniggering....

Sulu - 'With your Highness's permission ? May I carry on?' Prince Okamba glares at everybody and gestures gracefully for Sulu Wasei to continue:

 'The driver, after extensive questioning in the basement, has told me that he dropped the package whilst helping an old lady from the village of (consulting notepad) Swingle Matravers. Close to the old ladies cottage - It was raining. Hmm.   Yes....
'That's right!' said Lupie Shalmin desperately.

'But you said a Tramp ran away with it when you stopped your car!?' Piped up someone from the audience. Everybody, including Prince Okamba stares at the driver who shrivels up even further where he has been forced to stand. Prince Okamba makes a sign and one of the security guards lays a hand on the driver causing him to squeal. The driver is pulled back and sat down by the wall.

'Keep quiet or your punishment will be far worse than even You can imagine!' shouts Prince Okamba.
Lupie Shalmin shrinks back in his chair that he has been given. The embassy security man puts a hand on his shoulder again. Lupie looks up at this man mountain who

used to be quite friendly towards him... but no longer it seems. The bruises on the drivers back, partly administered by this gorilla in security uniform standing beside him, still livid on his back. His arms are sore from the beating he received earlier. A foretaste of what will come if Prince Okamba from the Royal Palace in Oshasha does not retrieve his parcel.

Sulu continues: ' I intend to go down to Dorset with a group of hand picked Embassy staff and recover our property...' He suddenly holds up a hand. Eyes swivelling round. Silence in the room. Looking at the far wall. All eyes follow his gaze. A faint scratching sound can be heard. Sulu goes to the wall. Prince Okamba gets down off his gilded chair and is beside Sulu in a second. Prince Okamba whispering. 'What is on the other side of that wall Sulu?'.
Sulu: ' An empty tenement your Excellency'.
Prince Okamba: 'Then why is there scratching? I thought I heard it earlier...'
Sulu: 'Cockroaches your Excellency'.
Prince Okamba: 'Oh! I see. (Sotto voce) We had those in the palace at Oshasha.
Sulu: 'I know. I slept in one of the beds's. I was scratching all night...'
Prince Okamba: 'You we're!? It's the heat'. Patting Sulu on the shoulder. 'Continue please..'

Sulu, clears his throat and turns; Prince Okamba steps back.

Sulu moving swiftly to the centre of the room again, but being careful to keep away from the chair and not block out Okamba's view of proceedings:
'Tonight we go in convoy to Dorset. And by the end of the week the secret device for forecasting the Gold Bullion stock market will be ours. Safe in the knowledge that none of the decadent Western countries will know what we are doing. Until it is too late, and we have them at our mercy. With that device we will rule the gold markets of the world and make Bahrun rich'.

Meanwhile on the other side of the wall in the supposed uninhabited tenement rooms, the scene, if the flaky Prince Okamba could have seen it would have sent him even further off his trolley than most people thought he was already. Hi tech probes attached to the wall, the secret services of four countries: England, France, America, and South Africa, all listening through headphones to Prince Okamba's conversation next door. Several sets of sophisticated recording equipment running.
One of the senior members of the British contingent moves away from the dividing wall and speaks first. His name is Mr Sydney Thomson - Jones.
'No doubt about it. They've found the device and then lost it again.

Frenchman: ' Having stolen it from us in the first place - they lose it again!'

American: ' I gotto phone this in to Washington. Then we've gotto get down there and find this damn thing before Bharun create another Wall Street crash!

Frenchman: 'You mean *our* secret device that *you* are looking for and which the French government will claim back - looking around at all the other people - whoever finds it..'

American: 'Sorry, Sorry! Yes the ah French device. Sure sure......
(moving away, sotto voce to his colleague) 'Jesus, how touchy can you get!'

The groups move further apart, the technicians packing up their portable equipment:

 Thomson - Jones sotto voce to a colleague: 'Get your people together for a meeting this evening please. We have to move quickly to steal a march on some of these characters'.

American to his colleagues over by the kitchen alcove, pulling across on a pole what remains of an old curtain: ' Don't hang around here. Get this gear packed up and get down to this Swingle Matravers place -wherever that is. Don't wait for nobody else!'.

Frenchman bent down round the back of an old settee whispering to his colleagues: 'We must get back the secret device for the honour and prestige of France! We leave tonight for Dorset. – Remember! We must stop at

nothing to get back what is ours. For the GLORY of the French republic!'
Colleague very much *off message*: 'But I thought it belonged to Bharun?'
First Frenchman: 'Keep your voice down!   But it belonged to France before the Bharunians got their hands on it. Remember!'.
'The Honour of France and 5000 francs travel expenses to every man if we recover the device before Saturday. 5 days time'.
Second Frenchman: 'Where will we stay? Which hotel? Weren't we told to watch our expenses on this trip?
First Frenchman: 'The best one going! Now come on - get that gear packed up, the others are almost finished'.

South African contingent - huddled behind an armchair and lamp standard. 'What are they all whispering about? How to get it back?'
 'Yes. But we're cleverer than them. We'll go down straight away. Get a head start. We can sleep in the back of the cars. We don't want to go mob handed though. Twelve of us should be enough. The backup can come down the day after tomorrow'.

London on a very wet rainy night.

The exit gates at the back of various London embassy buildings, and a certain large fortress like building down on the Thames. A lot of unusual activity. Shadowy people heading out towards cars and vans. Cars and vans leaving

fast. Drivers swinging through the gates and accelerating down the darkened back streets of London. Men inside the vehicles looking furtively out for signs that they are being watched by their rivals from other Embassies, or the British themselves. American, French, South African and Bharunian embassy cars all heading and converging on the main road south out of London. Jerky conversations going on in the diplomatic cars.   ' You think we fooled them?' I I think so. Wait! Isn't that the French? Looks like a diplomatic car behind?   No of course not. Who would use a Black Maria from the Embassy with a flag on it for a clandestine operation?'
The late night traffic is joined, streaming south out of the greatest metropolis in the world.

In the leading French Car. ' Don't you think we are conspicuous in such a large car? We use this one for visiting Buckingham Place!
'Nonsense': ' For the honour of France. Remember - the honour of France!
' I just thought we should not be so obvious'.
Senior man: 'Would Napoleon have skulked away in disguise when facing the enemy?? We have nothing to hide. Our cause is just. We are going to recover that which is rightfully ours from the hands of the English in their native Dorset'.
'Don't you mean the Bharunians?' This from a minion sat in the front seat next to the driver. He is ignored.

Claude the Embassy Driver for the first time - daring to
speak up while the dividing glass partition is still down -
' But surely we can take the French flag off the car sir?
It's the extra large one we use for visits to the Palace'.
'When we stop at a motorway service station perhaps'.
Driver: 'We're going into a motorway service station with
our French flag flying? This is a clandestine secret
operation Sir.
The head of the French task force leans elegantly back in
the white leather upholstery, smoking a cigar. ' You
know your trouble Claude? You have no style......'
Claude hurriedly presses the button the raise the partition.
Nobody wants to smell what the senior man is smoking.

The Americans.

The Americans had been following the French. This is not
difficult. A spy satellite had been stationed over the French
Embassy all evening, and every single movement down to
the size of a nat crawling across the window sill of the
French Ambassadors bathroom had been photographed.
Now the Americans and the other nations we're at a
motorway service station forty miles outside London. Late
evening. Complete farce ensures.

'Whaddya know? the Frenchies are here drinking coffee.
And look so are the Brits and the South Africans. Where's
the Bharun mob ? Anybody see them? They must not see
us'.

French: 'Look, it's the Americans! We should have sat further away. Look!, pointing a finger: The Bharunians...... So much for surprise'.
Various Embassy staff and the British are all using the toilets. Studiously avoiding each other and pretending they had not seen who else was there.

 A mass exodus to the cars follows. Everybody trying to avoid everybody else and not look in a hurry. Unfortunately the main entrance/exit to the car park is cordoned off with builders tape and low fencing due to overnight maintenance. A narrow fire door down the side of the building has been opened for people to go in and out to the car park. Everybody, Embassy and Security staff, public including prams and small children, all trying to squeeze through this one opening.
.

Interior of the Bharunian Embassy car; an old black maria.

Fifteen minutes later: Prince Okamba seeing other cars coming out of the exit slip road close behind them: 'Sulu I thought you said we would get down to the coast unseen?' Sulu: 'Driver! Lose them! Or it will be your head on the pole in the town square of Oshasha. They head off down the motorway and the car speeds up. Unfortunately, after some ten minutes they exceed the speed limit and are pulled up by the Motorway Police who we're observing traffic from a ramp three miles south of the exit slip road from the service station and have chased after them.

Police officer: '90 miles an hour Sir - this is not a race track'.

Sulu Wasei: 'We have Diplomatic Immunity officer. - this is His Highness Prince Okamba. On his way to a State Visit to Dorset'. Okamba sits up in the back, trying to look impressive. He fails. Dressed in drab clothes for this clandestine assignment, and looking for all the world like someone from a poor town with high unemployment. The car itself, with its bumps and scrapes looking like something from a road traffic accident, or several.

Policeman: 'Out of the car please'.

Sulu Wasei: 'Please officer we *are* in a hurry! Look at those other cars officer - pointing - they are going much faster than us!'.

Motorway police: 'It is <u>you</u> we are concerned about Sir'. The police examine passports and I.D. . A deliberately leisured consultation in their own car and then onto the police radio. Prince Okamba is dragged off protesting to sit in the back of the police car, where he is delivered of a long monologue on the subject of speeding. Eventually letting the Bharunian Embassy car and its occupants go. Along with the other car containing Embassy staff that had been following behind. All this has been very conveniently fed over the radio to the British security contingent following behind and having deliberately left it a while before leaving the service station themselves.

Meanwhile the American limo is passing the Bharunians:

Ist agent: ' Gee you see that!? The Bharuns got caught by the Brit police'. I'm sure it was them'.

'Let's hope it was nothing easy - watch your speed fella (this to the driver); we don't want to be next'.

Meanwhile in the Bharunian car as they, at last, speed away:

Prince Okamba: 'You think we got away with it?'.
Sulu WaseI: 'Does a Water Buffalo need water? - - I think so'.
Prince Okamba: 'If this goes wrong Sulu - your own head on the block in the market square at Oshasha. Not just the driver'. Sulu says nothing. The weight of success of this mission is clearly on his shoulders. And that of all his relatives back in Oshasha and the surrounding villages.

The cars speed on through the night.
Hours pass and the cars and vans of the security services are at last approaching the south coast of England - Dorset.

With the South African 's in their Embassy car, things aren't going too well.

Ist Agent: Leaning over from the back seat and trying to grab the road map: 'Where in the HELL are we?! That sign back there said Wareham - was it?! Where the hell is that?!

2nd Agent: 'Stop the car. We'll ask. There's a local over there'.

Unfortunately they have stopped by Mike Tomlinson, a local hood tough guy (when his wife isn't shouting at him) and who happens to be in his normal state - completely pie balled and rolling drunk. Chucked out of the pub in Wareham, the Crown and Anchor, and not wanting to go home and face the wife. Especially as she has been waiting up for him and its now 2 am in the morning. He'd been barred from the Drunken Cow in Swingle Matravers. As he had been for about a dozen other pubs in East Dorset.

Ist Agent being very polite: ' Excuse me Sir. We're trying to find where Swingle Matravers village is please?'
Mike: 'I live in Swingle - what's it to you!'
Ist Agent, still trying to be polite: ' Can you help us get there?'
Mike slurring his words: 'How much. What about a lish - ft?.
Ist Agent, dropping the smile: ' Get in'. Hands and arms drag him in.
The car continues down the road.
2nd Agent: ' How far is it then?'
Mike 'Get stuffed'. Promptly getting slapped across the face very hard for his trouble by the second agent leaning across the back seat. The agent looks like someone who participates in strong man courses and competitions when back at home.
Ist Agent: ' Leave it. We need to keep him alive'.
Mike: 'What is this!?'
2nd Agent producing a rubber truncheon.

'You know what this is?'
Mike eyeing up the truncheon: 'Christ - are you the Dorset police?'
Ist Agent (summing up Mike as a criminal): 'We're bank robbers and we want to know where Swingle Matravers is'
.

The agent saying this leans across and opens the car door threatening to throw Mike out. They are speeding along a very dark country lane towards Wareham.
Mike: 'All right All right. Keep your hair on! Why are you-all wearing dark glasses - can't you see or something?!'
The door opens even wider and Mike Tomlinson's head and shoulders are thrust out of the door. The rough tarmac and grit road is inches from his face. A shove and he bangs his fore head nastily on the road. There is a deep graze across the top of his head. Starting to bleed.
2nd Agent: 'Are you going to help or not?
Mike: 'Alright'.   Mike has sobered up very quickly.
Mike: ' Go straight on this road to Corfe Castle. Turn right where it says Swingle Matravers the other side. The place is two miles along.
The agent bangs Mike Tomlinson's right leg with his own truncheon. He howls with pain.
2nd Agent leaning across. 'Hope your right. Or you wife won't recognize you. Even less if you're a corpse'.
Mike: Who ARE you?! You don't have English accents.
The agents face is VERY CLOSE to Mike Tomlinson's ear.
Ist Agent. ' You work it out'.

Mike: You look like weirdos to me. Dressed all in black with those glasses. Are you from London? . He gets another thump on his leg for his pains. He howls with pain. The driver up front is grinning. Wishing he could join in.

Arriving at Swingle Matravers.

Ist South African Agent: 'Where's your house?'

They are passing the Drunken Cow public house and Mike tries to indicate with his uninjured arm and blinking blood away from his eyes. The graze to his forehead is now weeping blood in several places. He indicates that he's in one of the row of the unkempt looking terraced houses to the back of the pub itself. The car swings by round the back of the pub and up a rough looking road. This is not the part of Swingle that the tourists see. It is screened by trees. A shrill voice from an upper bedroom window. ' Keep the bloody noise down!. 3 o'clock. Where do you think you are?'

Ist Agent to Mike: ' We know now where you live now so keep your mouth shut. That includes talking to the police or your missus about this - get it?!'
The agent leans over, the car stops and Mike Tomlinson is shoved out the door onto the pavement, bruised and bleeding. He's left sprawled across the pavement with his neighbours Rottweiler yapping and snarling. All Mike can see through his haze of pain is a massive dog with

halitosis. Baring its teeth through a broken garden gate of the drug dealer living one door down from his own.

The South Africans are heading off up the road away from the houses.
Ist Agent: ' We need rooms to use as a base. Maybe the pub?'   'We should have thought about this before we left....' Guess we'll find something... or sleep in the cars tonight.

CHAPTER FIVE.
PLAN OF CAMPAIGN!

The different contingents have reached their hotels and guesthouses in Swingle. The South Africans have managed to hire two caravans next to each other on a field outside the village from a tenant farmer. The farmer being paid over the odds to keep his mouth shut about this sinister black garbed contingent turning up in two cars and van with blacked out windows. Knocking him up at 3 am to ask for accommodation.

The rest: the British, Americans, French, and Bharunians are all in the respective make shift accommodations arranged at short notice. A mix of the local pub, boarding houses, and a couple of back street private hotels in Swingle.

At the Drunken Cow public house in the early morning the Bharunian contingent are planning their day. Crowded into

the attic bedroom of Prince Okamba. Prince Okamba -
Bharuns greatest nut case - is holding forth. Imagining as
usual that everybody else is deeply interested in what he
has to say.
Sulu Wasei stands by what passes for an attic window.
Trying to stare out through the cobwebs and dirt streaks of
the single cracked pain of glass measuring about one foot
across.

Sulu and not Prince Okamba is the person really in charge
of the hunt for the secret stock market device, but no one
says this out loud. Sulu's face is bland and expressionless
as usual. Nobody really knows him, not even his wife, and
the children whom he plays with often when he is back in
Oshasha. Certainly not his wife's family from another
tribe and living about twenty five miles outside the
ramshackle Oshasha with its market place, posts in the
ground for executions and old French colonial buildings
pressed into service as the government headquarters. The
buildings themselves all but falling down.

Nobody in their right mind would want to live in Oshasha.
Not with the ruling Bharunian royal family in charge -
living as they did in the former District Governors house at
the end of the main street and in the carefully tended
grounds. With the magnificent gold painted high wrought
iron gates at the front. The palace a white washed edifice
standing behind.   A complete contrast to the rest of the
town.   The latter being infested with snakes and crocodiles
and whatever else encroached from the jungle at night.

King Obanda's imperial guard of thugs roaming the dirt roads at night with their dogs and rifles killing whatever came out of the jungle. This to protect both themselves and the populace which included the palace up the road. For this reason the population had a 10pm curfew to adhere to. Being out after dark risked being bitten by whatever came out of the jungle, but also being hit over the head by the guards themselves.   The last thing the victims we're ever likely to suffer in their too short lives under a bright African moon. Their bodies being thrown into a shallow pit out of town.

The only foreign embassy in town was a consulate run by the French. Everybody else, including the British and Americans had moved out to the neighbouring country of Uganda ages ago. The townsfolk having to go to a Ugandan first aid post and hospital on the other side of the border if they wanted any kind of medical help. A constant stream of people coming too and fro during the day time. Allowed through by the border guards who accepted bribes and who had to use the same facility themselves. No one in their right mind would accept the services of the Bharunian Army Medical Core. Go into their dark green army tent with the red cross on the top and you we're likely to come out with a leg or arm missing. Even though you went in their with nothing more than lacerations whilst using a machete to clear a path in the jungle on the orders of your Company Sergeant Major. The Bharunian Army using the same ranks as the British Army. The French Foreign Legion still trained in the jungle up to the far

North of the country and had their base there. But everybody in Oshasha ignored them. Occasionally the French could be seen in the town in their Kepi's and jungle uniforms trying to have a break from the camp. Standing around in the bars drinking the local hooch and looking out onto the dirt road that was the high street, but nobody spoke to them. Their foreign currency was accepted. The only bank in town the Bharunian National Bank of course, would accept it and exchange for the local currency the Bharan. But the inflation rate was so high the whole exchange rate mechanism was almost completely meaningless. Most people surviving on growing their own vegetables in their back yards. A pig and some hens in a small stockade made of old sticks tied together with wire or string pressed into the earthen floor. Disputes between neighbours when livestock went missing. Only settled by the army who accepted bribes from one side or the other to come to an adjudication as to who was the culprit. The latter having to apologise to his neighbour or get a beating.

Meanwhile in the attic bedroom in the Drunken Cow Prince Okamba was coming to the end of a long winded speech designed to rally his supporters in the room.
'- and so my brothers, we will go out and fight these ignorant people who slumber in their houses and walk around their village. We will enquire in all the shops and with the people. And if they don't answer.... a hot needle will soon loosen tongues.
Sulu: 'We cannot use torture here'.

Okamba ignores Sulu and with his head now lowered starts mumbling to himself. His voice growing ever louder. This alarms the entourage. Sulu hastily intervenes as a medical orderly from the Embassy and previously unseen at the back behind a curtain now moves forward to assist Okamba over to his bed. A makeshift cot in the corner.

Sulu: 'We must move. There are 12 of us now. The rest that arrived in the night from the Embassy are waiting and listening on the stairs outside. We will split into groups of 4 and scour the village. Do not make yourselves obvious. You must blend in with the locals. Drink their beer, eat their food. Be polite. Ask about the tramp that has been seen in the area but only after you have been in conversation for a while. Always be on the lookout for the gold bullion stock market forecasting device. You all know what it looks like? A rectangular black metal case, with lights and dials under a lid. About a foot and a half wide. Quite heavy. Should be in a canvas bag but that might have gone'. Sulu indicating with his hands the size and shape of the metal box as he speaks.

A chorus of agreement meets this last remark. 'You saw the pictures of it that I passed around?'. Then as an afterthought. 'The pictures show the device when it was new. It might be scuffed and scratched now but still recognisable'. Everybody nodded and tried to look wise and knowing at these remarks. All anybody wanted to do was get away from Okamba who was now lying down on the cot off to one side. Raving and mumbling to himself with his eyes staring at the ceiling and with saliva drooling from the side of his mouth. Being attended to by the Embassy medical orderly who had a syringe in his hand. Doubtless to subdue Oshashas' biggest nutcase!

As they leave the embassy doctor arrives from London and comes straight into the room and nods at the medical orderly whom he recognises. The doctor administers a further injection. Moments go by. Okamba lies comatose now on his makeshift bed. The doctor covering him with a rug and pulling his arms and legs out straight before leaving the room. Instructing one of the woman to sit in the room by the door and to let him, the doctor, know when His Highness awakes.

Sulu has been watching the proceedings as people are slowly filing out of the room and waiting on the stairs for any final instructions from Sulu who recollects himself and turns towards the stairs:
'Good, eat your breakfast quickly then. 9.30am - and we go. It is 7.30am.

Through the wall from the tenement attic next door and secreted in a cupboard the South African agents have heard it all.

In the bedroom, the two South African agents wrap up their listening equipment and conduct a whispered conversation.

Ist agent: ' 9.30? You sure?'
2nd agent: 'That's right Blitzing the town with their agents.
Ist agent: Will do it at 8.30am. It's 7.30 now. Let's eat.
2nd agent: 'What about the Americans?'
Ist agent: ' They'll still be in bed. They picked the best
hotel I hear.

The Grosvenor Hotel near the Pier entrance. Swanage
early morning. Conference room.

Men are standing around dressed casually, they hope, to
blend in. Communications being checked out. Enough
equipment for a small army going behind enemy lines to
observe from deep cover - or in this case round the backs
of houses in a picturesque Dorset village.
Lee Elroy - Meyers is the Deputy Head of Security at the
American Embassy. Lee's previous 'active service' was in
the Personnel Department at CIA HQ.
'Lee Elroy - Meyers: ' I told you boys. We're going to
whup these people'.
 The rest of the group mainly experienced CIA operatives
and a few newcomers to the Core are not too sure about
'whupping people' in a small time English village. In a
country that is their closest ally. A country moreover in
which they we're supposed to have, in theory at least,
some sort of special relationship. "Whupping people",
was not going to enhance it!

If the truth was known, quite a few of them, and the American contingent was a large one, we're not too sure about Lee Elroy - Meyers. But of course we're too diplomatic to say so. Certainly not to his face.

Harold Abrams a side kick to Meyers spoke up: 'You quite sure about this Lee?'
'Shuddup and just get the equipment operating. We don't want no foul ups'.
Harold (all ex USA Marine): 'Yessir! --. then pursuing his case:
'But when are we moving out Sir!? Everybody else will be either in Swingle or moving out of the hotels right now!'

Leon Starkey, another agent: lanky, sun burned, Stetson hatted Texan drawled:
'But the Bhar--unia–ns are already there Sir. They could be half way round the village - or worse. Found the goddam secret device AND making a fortune on the gold bullion stock market already! Suppose...' Lee Elroy: exploding with fury:

'What is the MATTER with you'll? Breakfast first, then we go. My stomach needs feeding'.

'So does your brain Meyers' thought Leon, but he said nothing out loud.
An emphatic chorus of: ' Yes Sir's!!' greets his reply to the breakfast call.

Lee Elroy: 'That's better. Now eat. The Bharuns and
everybody else can wait till later'.

They all glance at each with but a single thought. Who
get's it in the neck when Lee Elroy - Meyers screws up...
One thing was for certain. It wont be Meyers!'

CHAPTER SIX.
THE VILLAGE EXPECTS..

Outside the boy scout hut on the outskirts of Swingle
Matravers. Mid morning. Hot bright day. Prince Okamba,
rolling his eyes and looking madder than ever.

'Alright! We've been round the village once and seen the
market place. Now we interrogate the local people.
Sulu Wasei with disguised sarcasm: ' Hot irons your
Highness?!'
Prince Okamba taking him seriously: 'NO! We must be
more subtle. They do not go in for such methods here. At
least I don't think so'.

Sulu Wasei: 'My men know how to be subtle your
Highness'.
Prince Okamba: 'I hope they do...' Pointing at a thin
weedy looking boy of about 18 years of age.
'I see you have Xhosa with you. He was the one who got
high on drugs last year and tried to burn down the palace
at Oshasha!'. Pointing accusingly at Sulu. – - ' and YOU

have invited HIM to take part in this!? - I am surprised he is still walking about...'
Sulu Wasei soothingly. 'Xhosa is good medicine. He knows how to ward off the British evil spirits'. An ironic statement if ever there was one.
Prince Okamba, turning on Sulu Wasei again: ' What do you MEAN evil spirits?? Do I look like a primitive!? – you think I am ignorant peasant you frighten with your stories of evil spirits? You think...he spluttered on... you think you think. Eyes rolling, spittle dripping down from the side of his mouth.
Sulu Wasei trying to be calm: 'No No Your Highness.. Please do not alarm yourself, I can get the doctor again.. Or the medical orderly. He is still here from yesterday when you had your fit. The words we're out of his mouth before realising his error. Prince Okamba frothing at the mouth staring at him.

' You think to take my throne; to usurp my powers?? – You are in touch with Oshasha behind my back. YOU - flinging his arm out and pointing a long finger — seek to gain my position here in the Embassy!'
Sulu Wasei, now thoroughly frightened: 'No No your Highness, I would never do that'.
Okamba, eyes hooded and looking darkly at Sulu Wasei. 'There are ways of dealing with your sort. There are a lot of poisonous snakes in our part of Africa; and for a moment Okamba looks like a snake himself. A Black Mamba....or maybe an adult sized King Cobra....

'But for now I need you. Get the device back and all is forgiven. Fail me and...   Sulu forestalls anymore of this awful rhetoric by bowing low, almost touching the floor: ' I will not fail you your Highness - oh exalted and almighty one'.

This bogus flattery calms Prince Okamba who stops rolling his eyes for a moment. The assembled company breaths a sigh of relief. The madman, the beast of Oshasha is quiet once more. The Bharunian contingent led by Sulu Wasei leaves the public house. They are dressed in all manner of dark clothing topped off with sunglasses and trying to be inconspicuous in this picturesque thatched Dorset village. Locals going about their business look on with astonishment at this motley assortment. Assuming a film crew is in town again. The last lot was about a Sherlock Holmes Christmas special called: "The Witching Hour". Judging from the way these misfits seem to have been dressed by, they presume, the wardrobe department of the film company, maybe they are an extension of it.....?

The Americans just arriving in their cars see the Bharunians starting to fan out among the houses. Several of them approach the doors of the medieval looking thatched cottages. One of which is the front door of Mr and Mrs Hodges. Mrs Hodges is in the middle of cooking Sunday lunch. A small pugnacious woman in her late 40s, she appears at the front door wiping her hands on a tea cloth. She is not in a good mood at this interruption. An inviting smell of Sunday roast wafting through from the open kitchen door at the other end of the hallway.

Mr Hodges, a Foreman of one of Dorset County Council's Tarmac road mending gangs, and a man of few words, and most of those being grunts, is sat watching television in the front room. He is not known amongst his work colleagues, or around the village for that matter, for demonstrating the humorous side of his character. Unless that is, he is on the winning side of the pub darts team, or beating some hapless punter who'd had a few pints in an arm wrestling contest. Something that happens quite frequently. The loser having to buy the next round of drinks.

Mrs Hodges at the door: 'If your from the Donkey Sanctuary we took our jumble down there for the sale last week'. She peers up at the man half of whose face appears to be hidden behind huge black tinted sun glasses. Strange the people you get calling these days......-

Sulu Wasei: ' I am NOT from an animal sanctuary madam. I....
He got no further.
Mrs Hodges waspishly: Who are you then!? - I'm busy you know....
Sulu Wasei: 'I....
Mrs Hodges: If your collecting for the church we 'gave' last week.
Sulu Wasei: I am NOT collecting for the church!

Mrs Hodges stepping back slightly and turning her head: 'Arthur! Arthur! There's a man here causing trouble on your front door step! '

A creaking sound of an armchair groaning under the weight of its occupant as he levers himself upwards. A door opens. A veritable giant of a man emerges into the hallway from the front room. Moving slowly down the hallway towards the front door. The sun from outside completely blocked by his bulk.

Mrs Hodges: 'You see to him Arthur'. Stepping round her husband and crowding in behind.

Sulu Wasei smiles nervously upwards attempting to win over this giant Visigoth of a creature looking down at him through small eyes, a great suet pudding of a face and what appears to be mish mash of yellowed teeth. A smell of mothballs appears to permeate the air. An overfed tabby cat jumps in through the front door and runs past and off towards the kitchen to be greeted by cooing noises from Mrs Hodges.

Sulu Wasei in his best voice: 'Good morning Sir. We're helping the police to find a package that was dropped by accident in your village'. The view of Sulu Wasei, his mouth open, is abruptly cut off as Mr Hodges slams the front door in his face. He turns back to face his wife. There is not much intelligence in the eyes of this hulking great man. A once lively person in his youth, marriage and the cares of bringing up four children on a very limited income have drained it out of him. Being out in all weathers over thirty odd years has not helped either. 'I fixed him...' he grates in a low voice, moving away from the front door.

Mrs Hodges soothingly as though talking to a small child and holding the tabby cat to her chest:
 'That's right dear you fixed him; go back into the front room and watch TV. Yorkshire Pudding and all the trimmings today. Your favourite. Won't be long...'.
Mr Hodges grunts with pleasure and walks ponderously back into the bungalows neat small front room. The room is a silent testament to a long marriage and old enthusiasms. The Nicam Stereo TV . Shelves full of old film cameras. Ornaments bought from a dozen holidays to the Isle of Wight and places such as Ilfracombe, Minehead, Padstow and Tenby. Pictures of their four children and grand children adorn the walls.
A Ferguson record player topping a cabinet full of country and western LP's. Lamp standard with cream lampshade, chintzy curtains on pull strings by the windows. A small oval Waring and Gillows table under the window upon which Mrs Hodges over decorated artificial christmas tree would sit each year. Unwary christmas visitors sometimes tipping over the tree as one of the three ornamental legs of the table gave way as it was wont to do.

The room, north facing is cold and the long sofa sitting in front of the radiator blocking out the heat does not help. Neither do the curtains that fall down over the radiator blocking out what little heat does manage to struggle over the top of the sofa and into the room. A gas fire sits in the brown and cream tiled hearth near to Mr Hodges armchair located behind the wooden door. Tall bookshelves by the doorway lined with old book club editions of favourite authors; Agatha Christie, Dorothy L Sayers, E. F. Benson and others. Books indicating trips to W H Smith bookshop Swingle high street in the past years to buy essential items. Cookery books, photography, D.I.Y teach yourself books on carpentry, electrical, typing, economics, maths and English. Picture books on Hornby railways, the waterways, and books on airlines, BEA, BOAC. A legacy of their childrens interests in much younger days. Mrs Hodges several ring binders featuring magazines from the BBC Antiques Road Show. Burlington Mail order catalogues stack up the lower shelves and of which Mrs Hodges had been a long time Premier mail order agent. Monopoly and card games that only come out at Christmas time when their children visited. The games being kept in a glass fronted cupboard in the hallway, on top of which stood the trim phone.

A Granddaughter clock, very crudely made stands abandoned by the doorway. Its battery points rusted over. One of Mr Hodges earlier enthusiasms in this case for carpentry, since abandoned.

The volume of the TV goes back up. The commentary from Saturday afternoon football match. Domestic harmony is restored .....But not for long. The Americans have been stalking the Bharunians and saw what happened at the front of Mrs Hodges: cottage.

Lee Elroy - Meyers: ' No b-o-y-s that liddle old lady in that town shack obviously knows something or the Bharuns wouldn't have picked that place. Our job is to find out exactly what it is that the old lady knows'.

Lee Elroy - Meyers is dressed in white tuxedo and white brimmed hat. Just to look like he's blending in as a typical American tourist to little old Dorsetshire.

Ist agent: 'I'm worried sir. That lady was none to welcoming. I think we ought to leave it awhile. Maybe the public house will be open soon...

Lee Elroy - Meyers: 'Listen, when I want your opinions, which I don't, I'll ask for them'.

2nd agent: 'John's only trying to help Sir'.

Meyers: ' Butt out!' Exiting through the doorway.

2nd agent: ' Yes Sir!' The sarcasm is lost on Lee Elroy - Meyers. They walk off over to the cottage. Meyers knocks on the door and prepares to win over the lady of the house. He is about to wish he hadn't bothered.

Four agents are with Lee Elroy - Meyers. The other seven are moving up the road and knocking on doors. Trying to copy their esteemed leader.

The front door to Mrs Hodges house opens. Mrs Hodges now wearing a totally disbelieving expression on her face - is standing on the threshold. Down the hallway the football match can be heard in high action.

Brighton Rovers are knocking hell out of the opposing force namely third league Winchester Terriers. The football pitch looks like a slaughter ground with St John Ambulance Brigade volunteers running about the touch line with stretchers. An ambulance is making its way up the access road to where paramedics are tending someone under blankets. One of the Home side is being helped towards the ambulance that is approaching. Head and

football boots sticking out either end of the stretcher from under the blanket.
Local police stopping the hundred and fifty or so local spectators from knocking hell out of the visitors on the other side of the stands. Arthur is leaning forward in his armchair following it, wishing he was there, fist raised. One his friends from the road mending gang is on the terraces.   All this violence is getting his dander up.

Meanwhile at the front door Lee Elroy - Meyers stands there in all his glory
' how di-you-do to you ma-am!' raising his Stetson in greeting.
Mrs Hodges: Oh my good gawd - another lot'.
Lee Elroy - Meyers - ignoring the interruption - I represent the *American* Government Maam and I want to say what a proud pleasure and a privilege it is to meet you this fine morning. I...
Turning her back on Meyers, Mrs Hodges marches back down the hallway into the front room. She demonstrates by her next words exactly how well you can deal with bothersome callers in the Hodges household.
'Arthur! Arthur! It's another lot of people come to disturb your television. And the Sunday lunch is about to go on the table. Your favourite, Yorkshire Pud and Roast beef. – *When* I can get to the kitchen to serve it to you with all these interruptions.
Arthur, deep in the match, heaves himself up from his armchair and lumbers out of the front room, down the hallway to the front door. A nasty expression on his face.

Lee Elroy - Meyers: 'Well how-de-do Sir, and a fine morning it is. Me and my friends here were just wondering if you could just spare us a moment of your so valuable time on this grand morning to....

Arthur Hodges with absolutely no sense of humour grips the jacket of Lee Elroy - Meyers. Heaving him up three feet and physically throwing him backwards into the street towards the rest of the party.

Arthur Hodges grunts, turns, shakes his shoulders, jerks his fore finger at the rest of the group and walks back into the cottage slamming the door. The Americans pick Lee Elroy - Meyers up off the road where he has landed on his bottom.

Lee Elroy - Meyers: 'Weel - seems they don't seem too friendly round here, lets get to that Post office. Maybe the lady in there - what's her name (consulting list), are yes a Mrs Travers the Post Mistress. Quaint title. See if she's more amenable'.

Meyers walks unsteadily up the high street trying to regain what little dignity he has left. Accompanied by his posse. There approach is observed by the: Vicar, the Butcher, the Baker and others all out in the high street. All these men coming up the road in their dark glasses and their dark suits except for there leader who appears to be wearing something out of a stage musical.   Maybe they are tourists and can be tapped for money? The local Dorset accent gets thicker. The American enters the post office just as about half the village decide that they too need to buy stamps, newspapers and sweets for the children.

Ist agent whispering: I don't think this is a very good idea Lee Elroy. This is supposed to be an undercover operation and *your* asking the Post Mistress in broad daylight whether she's seen a secret device in a brown paper parcel?!

Lee Elroy - Meyers: ' Do you take me for an idiot?'

Ist agent: ' Ah well — no sir. But I do think there are better ways of doing this'.

Lee Elroy - Meyers: 'Thanks!'

A chorus of comments from the other agents of: - 'Just trying to help'. And 'That's right'.

Meyers: ' If you want to help, get back there and search the village - with the rest of our people'.

Mrs Travers, busying herself below the counter. She is also a member of Swingle's 'Committee for Wealth'. Has heard about the Americans and is well aware of what the rest of the weirdo's skulking round the village are after. Her own daughter, recently married and living in one of the new houses on the council estate had been door stepped by one of these people and had just rung her mother up about it. Not too mention a warning phone call the previous evening from fellow committee member Jane Driver .

Mrs Travers , Post Mistress, early 40's and who has spent her life dealing with the clueless at the counter. It's looks as though she is about to deal with a few more. Even if they are CIA in disguise.

Mrs Travers comes from behind her post office grill in the darkest corner of the newsagents and stands behind the

general counter with it's sweets, magazines and newspapers. Putting on a sickly smile: 'Can I help you?'
Lee Elroy - Meyers, raising his hat in what he thought of as an old fashioned British way: 'We–ll yes indeed m-a-a-m I really hope you can. You see we wondered whether you've had any parcels through here for posting today. Perhaps an odd triangular shape and heavy?
Mrs Travers: ' No. Doesn't ring any bells to me' . She stares implacably at the Americans. The smile gone.
Lee Elroy - Meyers: 'We're just asking around - do you know of a man of the road, a Hobo, as we'd call him, by the name of Henry?'
Mrs Travers: ' Yes I know Henry. Saw him last week. Goes up to the Salvation Army hostel in Swingle for a wash and that.
Lee Elroy - Meyers: ' Where exactly is this place maam?'
Mrs Travers: ' Up tather end of the High Street - near the church'. Pointing through the open door up the road. The upper part of the church spire seen dimly through the buildings and clutter of the high street.
Lee Elroy - Meyers raising his hat: 'Thank you kindly maam. W-e-e-l-l go up their directly'.
The Post Mistress nods and raises a hand at them. They leave.
Villager whispering urgently: 'Why didn't you tell him that Henry is always drunk and never says anything to strangers. Likely to *hit* them more like than *talk* to them....

Mrs Travers is looking out of the narrow wire reinforced side window by her postal counter, giving a view of the pavement. She said, almost to herself: 'Let them find out for themselves'. They'll learn...

Meanwhile in the Church grounds at the very end of the village high street the Reverend Charles West is standing with Fred Driver and Bill Hutchings. They are hiding away from view in the doorway of the Vestry. Reverend Charles , a worldly wise person whose been around and then some. Tall and scholarly. Much revered by the locals for his prowess with the darts team when assisting at the Drunken Cow when the local pub tournaments are on: '
Do you suppose there onto the tramp Henry?'
Bill Hutchings: 'Possibly, he won't tell them anything though'.
Fred Driver: ' How can you be so sure?'.
Bill Hutchings: ' I bribed him'.
Reverend Charles West: ' You did what?!'
Bill Hutchings: ' Bribed him vicar. With ten packets of herbal cigars'.
Reverend Charles West: ' Those disgusting things?! –
Isn't Linda Dodswell making those for people who insist on smoking in the bath?'
Bill Hutchings: That's right Reverend. Only the tramp don't take baths as a rule. Just smokes them in the street. Or, he added with feint maliciousness, in your church vestry vicar...! – when that curate of yours isn't looking...
Reverend Charles West: ' There's been a smell recently in there must admit. Like old boots....

Bill Hutchings: 'That's it Reverend! That's why Linda says they should only be smoked in the bath. Away from everybody else like!'.

Fred Driver looking up the high street with his binoculars : 'Will you both stop going on about Linda Dodswell's latest foul concoction. ' The Americans are going into the Sally Army hut. Closely followed by the Bharunians by the look of it'. What do they think they look like? Dressed in black with sunglasses. Bound to put the Sally Army on it's guard... - who's on today anyway? '

'Piddle. Ex Warrant Office, now Captain in the Salvation Army - and his long suffering wife Linda'. Says Bill.

Fred: 'They still together? Thought they separated for good. She must have the patience of a saint to stick him'. Giving her, her orders every morning. Both of them standing to attention by the kitchen table as he reads out from a typed list. Gawd..!'

Reverend Charles West: ' Heaven help the Americans when they meet him - all I can say!'. Though, he reflected, that was an unchristian thing to say. He would pray for forgiveness later....

CHAPTER SEVEN
THE SALLY ARMY.

The Salvation Army Hut near the church, early afternoon. A small church army band is playing outside the entrance to a large wooden former scout hut that had seen better days. The hut painted and patched up more times than most people could remember. The back of it propped up with bulks of timber. This to stop it disintegrating through the hedge into a well tended back garden beyond.

The hut measures about 30 feet long by 15 feet wide. Inside the walls have been painted in Mahogany with a small dais at one end adorned with a made up wooden cross, nailed to a pedestal and covered with brass drawing pins to aid ornamentation. The Cross coming from a person who lived on a housing estate in Northampton in the Midlands. Collected by an elderly couple that had been prevailed upon to make the long journey to the persons house to Northampton to pick the thing up. Getting there, peering at street maps late at night and navigating around the back end of an unfamiliar town in the cold and wet with the windscreen wipers constantly going in their 1970s Vauxhall Victor car. Peering out at one darkened street after another, there had been a power cut in the town. The drive there had not been fun. When they'd finally got to the house, in the furthest corner of one of these cul de sacs at 9 o'clock at night, the man, a widower, had forgotten they we're coming and was having a bath. Manhandling the Cross, all four foot of it and heavy, into the back of their car with the back seat down had not been fun. Especially as the man himself, standing shivering in his dressing gown inside his garage, had been unable to help.

On subsequent visits to Dorset the elderly couple had not volunteered for anything more than community singing with the brass band!

Back in the hut an old fashioned organ stood to one side, a lever sticking out at the side connected to bellows. The lever being pulled up and down to pump air through the organ pipes.

Incomers, usually got lumbered with this task. Brash types usually - all mouth and money living in barn conversions with tinny looking 4 by 4's as their runabouts. Loud mouth woman with bawling kids who'd thought they could get the better of the locals. The Post Mistress whose daughter actually played the organ for the Salvation Army church services, would suggest with an innocent becoming smile on her face to the incomer, that they pump the organ for a bit to see what it was like. Finding out too late that the rudimentary set of organ pipes required a lot more pumping to get air through them going than the unsuspecting newcomer ever realised. But by then of course it would be far too late as the service had started anyway. They had to stand there and pump away looking like a complete prat to the rest of the congregation. And since the services we're not exactly short - the Salvation Army liked to give value for money - the person concerned would often find that they we're lumbered with standing there for well over an hour. Usually in a massive draft from the rotted timbers at the back of the hut.

The pipes of the organ led up towards the suspended ceiling. This being a very polite term indicating the discoloured and badly fitting polystyrene tiles that hung down on a rusted network of wires. The tiles themselves, mostly discoloured from age and roof leaks. Doubtless some thick individual who did general carpentry and electrical work would be prevailed upon to make a good impression by fixing everything for free. If they could find someone gullible enough that is, to believe that such efforts would stand them in good stead with the locals (they hadn't met many of them yet!).

Salvation Army Captain Lawrence Piddle and his merry helpers stood near the entrance resplendent in their Salvation Army uniforms. Trying to shelter from the rain during this 'Open Day' for members of the public. 'Open Days' being set up whenever the village looked swamped with tourists, and ostensibly for those who wish to come along and join the Church Army. Doubtless to make a generous donation before they leave in return from being sheltered from the Dorset weather.

Inside near the entrance, trestle tables are covered with pamphlets about the Sally Army and local charities and arts and crafts. Patriotic flags adorn the walls. Down one side is the tea urn steaming away and operated by volunteers doing a roaring trade. Helped largely by the poor weather outside that is driving people through the door. Assorted members of the public and passing tourists sitting around on the thin tubular stack up chairs with canteen type folding tables some covered with plastic table cloths and covered with sugar and salt cellars and assorted plates with rock cakes, sandwiches wrapped in cling foil and partially opened, cakes and biscuits for the children to eat. Drinking tea out of plastic cups. The rock cakes going particularly well.   "Got a good dentist have you" being a frequent off quoted remark to a tourist by a passer by about to put half a rock cake into his mouth.

A jumble sale of donated clothing and assorted bric a brac spread out on decorators tables down the side. Presided over, as ever, by the Reverend Charles and his wife Paula with their happy band of helpers. Arts and Craft stalls selling an assortment of locally sourced items presided over by the tradesmen who had obtained them. 'Locally sourced' being a rather elastic term. Imported through Liverpool Docks might give a more accurate picture.

No one had mentioned any of the above of course to Lee Elroy - Meyers when he and his posse had been directed to the Salvation Army Hut by the guardian of the local Post Office!

 Meyers and his slightly strange group of men in dark suits and sunglasses approach the scout hut entrance. They are almost immediately seen as potential converts to the cause. They get all sorts coming through the door.....and the Church Army are desperate for new recruits. Well just desperate really.....

Greeting them is Captain Lawrence Piddle, previously in the part time Territorial Army Catering Core as a Warrant Officer. After leaving the regular army as a catering core

NCO.   But now doing 'Gods Work' in the Salvation
Army. Carrying their rank of 'Captain'. Known to many
in the as old 'Piddle' or piffle, as that was what he was
largely credited as actually talking most of the time.
' Good afternoon, gentlemen, have you come to learn
about OUR work?'. Piddle adopting a pious attitude.
Lee Elroy - Meyers: 'Well to tell the truth, we're looking
for someone..'
He is faced by the confusing ranks of the Salvation Army
of which he knows nothing.
Captain Lawrence Piddle assuming an even more pious
attitude. Hand striking a vague attitude of prayer or
salutation:
' Yes we are all here on GODS work - may I give you a
pamphlet?'
Lee Elroy - Meyers: 'Thank you Sir, what we wondered
was - have you seen a local down and out by the name of
Henry? We don't know his last name'.

Piddle, as though about to indicate divine intervention: '
Many people prefer to remain anonymous in this world.
Then more sharply: 'Why exactly do you wish to contact
Henry?'
Meyers: 'W-e-e-l **Sir**, we believe he can help us find some
kind of lost property...
Piddle: ' And you think he has it?'
Lee Elroy - Meyers: 'W-e-e-l ... – it's just possible. I
mean an item of great value. I mean, that is, to the right
people'.

Piddle: 'And you wish, assuming an even more pious air, if that we're possible, - to enlist the Church Army in your quest? Adding hastily: ' Of course we will try and help you but our expenses in running this elaborate operation, an arm sweeping around the hut with its metal chairs and decorators fold up tables. The separate jumble and catering operation with its plastic cups and home made rock cakes. Does mean that we rely entirely on donations from our wealthier visitors. (Pointedly looking at the Americans expensive suits as he says   it).
Lee Elroy - Meyers: 'Well we would of course be willing to make a donation to your cause-----'.
 'Shall we say $2000.00 dollars ?
 Meyers blanches at him, he'd been thinking of more like 30 dollars but pays over the money from a brief case one of his group is carrying. 'Now if you could just tell us where we can find Henry - we'll be on our way'.

Piddle ever more piously: 'Alas the person who can tell you that is not here at present, but will be joining us soon - in another hour. So (coming a lot more down to earth in his manner) if your group of helpers would like to assist us with the jumble sale at the other end of the room? Also we are short of ladies to help with the tea. So if you gentleman could assist....
Lee Elroy - Meyers exasperated: 'But I thought you knew.....' he got no further.
Piddle raising his eyes to heaven in a grotesque parody of the clergy: 'It is all in Gods hands; and now if you would like to honour your promise to help us this afternoon?...

that is what Mrs Travers, our revered post mistress said to
me on the telephone just now you we're here to do.   This
is an exaggeration but Meyer does not know this. What
Mrs Travers had actually said was: " Watch out for the
weirdos with suits coming down the road..."

Meyers throws his hands up in the air, tries to ignore the
dark mutterings of his agents. Outside the rain continues
to pour down. People enjoying the pleasant stroll in the
high street or by the River Frome, are now barging in with
their umbrellas to escape the deluge. If not soaked to the
skin already. Looking for anywhere at all that is under
cover and has a heater. The holiday brochures always
showed sunshine....
Meyers talking back to his team. 'I can see it's raining ! –
Get serving the tea and cakes dammit! Jesus wept! – and
bring me some as well. I'll be sitting over there. Pointing
to an empty table and camping stool near a portable
electric radiator. All that was left to sit on.

Captain Lawrence Piddle hearing all this: ' If you just go
and see the Reverend Charles West at the other end of the
hut, he will tell you what to do. Signalling with his arms at
the Rev West over the backs of their heads as move over to
where the Vicar is standing with his wife. Meyers
authority diminished, trailing behind his agents, clearly
wondering why he had not left all this to one of his
deputies on the team. Just stayed back looking at
paperwork, leaving the action to others in the field.. What
he'd always done best in Personnel....

We leave the scene of the jumble sale, which helped by the weather is now in full swing and the 'happy helpers' from the American Embassy are being harangued by the local villagers looking for bargains amidst all the bric a brac.

Meanwhile the Bharunians led by Sulu Wasei are having to account for their lack of success to Prince Okamba who has arrived to hear progress in finding the tramp. Prince Okamba looks as though he would like to roast his people in boiling oil.
' So you have not been able to find this Henry person?! - he must be in the village somewhere. Find him!'
Sulu Wasei: But your Royal Highness - my men have looked everywhere. Where else do you suggest we look?
 'You expect me to do the job for you?!'
Sulu Wasei: ' No . no your Highness - it is just that we are all very tired now and...
Prince Okamba interrupting, eyes wide and staring:
'Plenty of time for you to sleep when you are in your grave...' The rest of the group visibly back away from Sulu Wasei.
Prince Okamba looking round him: 'The rest of you will not escape my wrath'.
'You will keep looking until it is dark. I have been watching the Americans, the English and the French and South Africans. The village is swarming with them! The Americans have been asking around. The South Africans have been searching the other villages as well as this one, but they have found nothing! As far as I can see anyway.

Sulu musing out loud as to where the South Africans are now.
 Prince Okamba pointed his stick. ' You should know where all these people are! They are the enemy and YOU! are the Head of Intelligence in this country for our people living here. YOU! will be the first to be called to account when we are all back in Oshasha'.
Sulu Wasei pretending to fawn in front of this madman from Oshasha: 'We will search all night for this man your ROYAL Highness (bowing low in mock obeisance). 'No stone will be left unturned. I will personally hold myself responsible for finding this man. If he is here in the village then we will find him'.
Prince Okamba looks at Sulu Wasei as though through the hooded eyes of a venomous snake that his ornate cane stick with its snake motives represented. The expression on his face is frightening. His next words are appropriately hissed:
' I am so glad that you said that Sulu - my brother His Majesty King Obanda the 3rd - - may heaven bless him - be most reassured to hear you say that. My secretary will communicate with him this evening, from my hotel!

- I will leave you now (raising his voice to the group). Four of you will remain to help Sulu - the rest can return to the public house and their rooms.
Another venomous look at Sulu Wasei as he leaves with his entourage. Tapping the driver on the shoulder with his stick.   Half the village appears to be packed into the scout

hut, fascinated by these scenes of how an African leader deals with his people. Amazingly Prince Okamba does not appear to have noticed any of them. Such are his mental preoccupations.

Sulu Wasei watches the car in silence from the pavement, keeping his thoughts to himself. Turning back towards the village and the now closed butchers shop belonging to John Hobson. It is still pouring with rain. The pavements are wet and the roadside drains running with water where cars have been throwing up sheets of water. Some of the drains are blocked and water overflowing onto the pavements in places.
Thunder can be heard. Distant lightning flashes across the sky. It all fits in with the mood that Sulu Wasei is in. The Americans, and for all he knows the French and the British are under cover in the same damned village. In the warm and dry. But what they we're doing God only knew. For he surely didn't! He, the Head of Bharunian intelligence in Great Britain was getting soaked talking to a lot of annoyed locals who clearly did not want to talk to him! Who, in all honesty, could blame them.

He marches towards the shop, the others following and picking up his lead and attitude. Getting ready with grim determination to do whatever was necessary when inside.

Reaching the butchers shop Sulu turns and gestures abruptly to them and pointing: 'You two! Round the back in case he tries to escape. The other two follow me'.

Two of the younger men with Sulu peel off and run off down a side alley.

Inside his comfortable apartment above the butchers shop, John Hobson is watching BBC 9 o'clock news. David Waring the main anchor man is just talking about strange goings on in a Dorset village with John chuckling to himself and just reaching down for his pint glass when he hears a strange noise downstairs. Footsteps on the bottom stairs.

Remembering that he had not locked the outer utility room door from the yard he turns out the lights and picking up a poker goes silently across and out of the door onto the landing and down the stairs. Reaching the bottom step he raises the poker, but before he can do anything his arms are pinioned behind him by someone who appears to resembles the size of a gorilla. The poker clatters harmlessly to the floor.

Out of the darkness comes Sulu's voice silky with menace. ' I hope this is not an inconvenient moment to talk to you Mr Hobson. We bring you greetings from Bharun. – perhaps we can all go upstairs ....?' John, a big man struggles heavily but is no match for the gorilla holding him and is slugged over the back of the head. Half carried half pushed upstairs he is dumped in an armchair and a small table lamp switched on by his captors. Groggily he sees a slim build man in dark clothing, Sulu Wasei, sitting in the half darkness in front of him. The others in the shadows behind. Silent and menacing. They hold kaboks, rubber truncheons, using for beating people.

Sulu Wasei in a quiet persuasive voice: ' I need your co-operation Mr Hobson. It appears you know where some property of ours is hidden. Before we leave , you are going to tell us where it is'.

John Hobson: 'Like hell I am!'   He is rapped on the arm with a kabok by someone standing behind him. It hurts badly. John grunts with pain.

Sulu Wasei: 'Please don't take that attitude Mr Hobson, my people are quite good at getting information from people. It would not take them long I can assure you. You would not be the first to talk'.

John decides to play for time: 'What do you want to know'.

Sulu Wasei: 'That's better. You see we don't want to hurt you but we have asked all round your village to find out about the elusive Henry, but the villagers are not talking. ' but YOU certainly will be'.

John: ' Well?

Sulu: ' Where is Henry?

John: ' Couldn't tell you. He left the village some days ago. He doesn't live here. Wonders the roads' . Sulu Wasei produces a gun with a silence fitted. ' It's quite simple - we start with your legs and arms and then move on to other parts'. To reinforce his point two bullets hit the cushion inches away from John's head. Sulu Wasei: ' Well?'

John, shaken, decides to adopt a cringing tone in his manner and voice: ' I can take you too him if you want, but please, please, don't hurt me!'   He cringes and snivels grotesquely Unbeknown to anyone in the darkness of the room his left hand has slid down into the crevice of the large old armchair he is sitting in. His fingers close around a pager device. . Pressing a silent panic button on the pager itself. He withdraws his hand. Part of the village pager system connecting with the other members of the Committee for Wealth and the Police. This action has gone completely unnoticed by the others in the darkness. Such is the writhing and cringing about that John has been doing. Moving his arms and legs about constantly whilst he was doing it.

In houses and cottages across Swingle a muted buzzing noise is heard as people sit watching television, in the kitchen or dining rooms or out in their garages and sheds. This includes Fred and his Wife Jane in their large farmhouse on the pig and cattle farm.
Fred reaches down reads the name of the person sending the signal, pressing the silent acknowledge button before getting up and reaching for his coat, telling his wife he has to go out and why. Reaching for the phone to call the police. Similar actions are happening elsewhere. Linda Dodswell moving towards the phone and calling into the kitchen to say that John Hobson is in danger and that the pager has just gone off. Bill Hutchings the Chemist in his bungalow looking at his pager and then heading for the door, grabbing his hat and coat and a stoat walking stick as he passes. The Reverend Charles West looking at his pager and calling the police, this time Special Constable John Mc Turk (a local part time volunteer). Telling McTurk what

has happened before shouting to his wife up the stairs, and leaving the house. Hurrying to his car.

Inside the apartment above the butchers shop Sulu Wasei is getting ready for a little of the
type of interrogation that goes on only in the back of the kitchens behind the high walls of the Kings Palace in Oshasha.

Sulu Wasei now *very* threatening with his gun. 'You will take us there now!'. John playing for time. ' Cold night. I'll need to get my coat'.   Sulu Wasei looks as though he just wants to throw the Butcher down the stairs.   They all move towards the door. Two of the Bharunian thugs moving up behind John pushing him forward : ' No tricks. Unless you want your skull cracked open'.
 ' I can assure you I don't want that!' Still cringing and backing away realistically. John stumbles down the stairs, prodded all the way by the two thugs. As they reach the bottom of the stairs and back door John glimpses an outline of a car with police markings. It was not there before. He goes straight to the door and flings it open, throwing himself quickly to one side, leaving the others behind him exposed. Sulu Wasei - jostled forward by the two thugs behind is blinded by arc lamps. A policeman's voice: 'Armed police' 'Stand still - get on the ground. Legs and arms apart'. Sulu Wasei darts through the door and attempts to run for it. It's a bad mistake. A hail of bullets and Sulu Wasei goes down, hit in the chest and legs. Crack, crack, crack crack, and again crack! The

two thugs scream and grunt in pain. Falling backgrounds in the doorway. Being dragged out along the ground by the police. Roughly searched for weapons and handcuffed to await medical attention.   The two that we're round the back have already been caught and are in the back of a police van.   One has leg wounds being bandaged up by a paramedic from the ambulance. The police rush in and go over the property.   Crowding up the stairs shouting warnings to anybody hiding there.

 Members of the 'Committee for Wealth' approach John slapping him on the back and offering congratulations.

Fred Driver: 'The police are to going to want to know what happened John . I'll talk to them with you.
 'You can make a statement but it's me they'll want Fred' said John.
Superintendent of Police one Frank Harmer approaches them. 'We know what they we're looking for - you want to tell us where it is - this 'secret device' of theirs that creates such a fortune on the stock exchange?'

Fred Driver puts his arm round Frank's shoulder. He's known him for many years since Primary School.
'It's like this Frank - let me tell you a story about an impoverished third world African country that likes to behead people on market day. How they came here to test their device on us innocents in Dorset. How's the missus by the way... I've got the latest batch of Jane's Elderberry wine upstairs. I'm sure John wont mind sharing it with

you. If your off duty now perhaps you and your Sargent
would like to sample some of it. Perhaps take a bottle
home.....!?' John nods his assent. 'Have you thought what
your going to be doing after you retire Frank, says Fred.
Always a place for you here on the Committee for Wealth.
Thought of doing a bit smuggling maybe....?
The Superintendent gives him a sharp look and raises his
eyes to the sky as they enter the butchers shop. It's going
to be a long night getting the statements he needs. He can
see that......

Next Morning:

At the very grand looking sprawling Grosvenor Hotel,
Swanage, the American contingent having breakfasted in
the ornate dining room are now in the equally ornate
conference room discussing the situation. The entire team
of thirty people are there.   The main man Lee Elroy -
Meyers is still convinced that the device has been hidden
by the villagers of Swingle Matravers somewhere nearby.
The obvious choice being Corfe Castle, a very ancient
monument a few miles away and shrouded in mist most of
the time, it seems to Meyers.
 'W-e-e-l fellers, since the device is nowhere around here
we have to widen our search. A good place I–m a thinking,
is that it's buried over at the castle ruins. Don't suppose
Maid Marian would have minded...
The others just look at each other blankly and shrug their
shoulders...

Meyers points at a large tourist map on the wall showing all the local attractions'.

Ist agent: ' So what do you suggest Sir?'

 Meyers: ' Seems to me that the person who does know about this is one of these:

' Committee for Wealth' people. I suggest the Chairman of the whole thing. The head honcho himself, Fred Driver.

2nd agent: ' He runs a pig farm just outside Swingle Matravers and ......

' I KNOW that he does dammit! I just said I thought we ought to visit him is all!'.Meyers het up now that all the pressure is bearing down on him for a result.

Ist agent: 'Right now Sir?'.

Meyers: ' You got something on....?'.

2nd agent: 'It's just that we've all been going since the break of day - maybe we could get some food?'.

 Meyers: 'You people – always thinking of your stomachs...Look at me - fit as a flea. Working out in the gym everyday'. The others look at their bosses beer belly, sallow faced complexion and crabbed feet. Their disbelieving looks show that they don't think their boss has been anywhere near a gym in ten years.

Lee Elroy - Meyers: 'We're going round to that pig farm right now. If necessary we're going to bust in on them and force it out of that farmer exactly where the device is. We're going to whup him good'. Thumping the table as he says this..

Ist agent: ' Don't you think the Brits will object Sir, I mean this is Great Britain, not some hick third world state'.

Lee Elroy - Meyers: ' You find me someone here in this here Swanage or Swingle Matravers or hoosit where Fred Driver's pig farm is and we'll get out there right now'.

Ist agent: 'As it happens there is a lady staying at this hotel who knows him. Her name is - consulting note book - Eleanore Wright. Mrs Eleanor Wright. Apparently she's some sort ah older half sister to Mr Driver. But I should say that in the early days.......'
Meyers interrupts:
' I don't want a history lesson God dammit!   Just get hold of her and we'll go find this dammed pig farm. Pick her up on the way'.

Eleanore Wright is doing her shopping halfway down the high street and at this moment just coming out of the chemists shop, talking to the owner Bill Hutchings as she leaves. Eleanore is 75 and very hard of hearing. In her younger days a feisty woman who had a reputation for taking on the local council and righting wrongs on behalf of others who could no longer cope. A bit of a busy body but her heart was in the right place as it we're. Although now elderly, she has retained some of that attitude. Council workers, even today, being wary of her appearance in their offices.

Chatting to Bill Hutchings in the shop doorway of Hutchings Chemists. Turning as she negotiates, with Bill's help the two centuries old worn stone steps leading down onto the pavement from the shop doorway.

Bill smiles and says goodbye before turning to go back
into the shop, just as the Americans draw up in their
limos. They jump out, grab hold of Mrs Wright and
attempt to drag her into the back of the lead car . Eleanore
is distracted looking into her capacious handbag and
thinking she has left something in the shop. Now
suddenly, some idiot in dark glasses is trying to get her
into a large car with aerials sticking out and blackened
glass on the windows. Bill Hutchings turning at the
commotion staring at the scene unfolding on the crowded
pavement with people walking past. Three large men
trying to manhandle an elderly lady into the back of a car.
Bill is surprised to hear a polite western drawl coming
from some person with a huge white hat who looks like
Larry Hagman from the Texan TV oil soap "Dallas".

Meyers raising his ten gallon hat: 'Hello maam, my name
is Lee Elroy - Meyers and I would be grateful for your
assistance in finding your half brother Mr Driver'.
Eleanore is struggling with the sensitivity (volume) control
on her hearing aid whilst fending off the three suited yobs
with their dark glasses.
She is trying to increase the hearing aid volume from 3 to
8. In her agitation she has turned it down to 2.
Consequently she has not heard a word of what this weirdo
in a white caramel suit and a big hat and dark glasses is
trying to say to her. To make matters worse it is refuse
collection day in Swingle and a big refuse lorry has just
stopped nearby making a tremendous racket as its rear

bucket mechanism moves constantly up and down tipping trade waste from the shops into the back of the truck. Two refuse workers moving up and down the pavements pulling the bins to the back of the lorry and then replacing them empty down round the back of the shops. Also pop music blaring out of a portable radio from teenagers on motorcycles who had stopped in the bus space ten yards away.

Mrs Wright: ' What? Who ARE you!'. Who are you....!!'
It's no good though, she still can't hear a word.
Lee Elroy - Meyers in his best polite public speaking voice: ' We are part of a group of people from America trying to locate something that belongs to us. We need your help, on behalf of the President of the United States.

Mrs Wright screwing up her face and staring at him. The refuse lorry going full tilt nearby, with its high pitched whining noise, clattering and banging as the bins lift up and down at the back.

' I don't know <u>what </u>your going on about young man!'
Says Mrs Wright, very annoyed now. A group of bystanders is gathering to watch this interesting spectacle. Like something in the films this is. Some reaching for their cameras. Meyers ignoring the growing crowd jerks his arm and some his men grab Mrs Wright once more who promptly screams:. ' Fetch the police! I'm being abducted!!' A young woman with a child in a buggy:

'Oooh! It's like something off telly!' Mrs Wright starts hitting Lee Elroy - Meyers with an umbrella . 'Will no one come to my aid?'.

Meyers: 'You've got it wrong Mrs Wright, we only want to get you in the back of the car. Oohs and Aaahs from the crowd.

A large swarthy man from the crowd tries to intervene but is manhandled away by two of the men in dark glasses. The mans friends weigh in, soon the security posse are outnumbered as all manner of comments and oaths are shouted at the Americans. 'Bloody yanks. Piss off home. Keep your hands off our women. We remember the war round here– when you lot we're over'. And a lot more in the same vain. Police sirens can be heard in the distance. Mrs Wright is still attempting to hit the Americans with her umbrella who finally manage to drag her into their car. A huge fight going on outside on the pavement. All manner of people, men, women, and teenagers, most of whom have no idea what its about, all throwing punches at each other and the people in dark glasses. Stones being thrown at the cars.

Lee Elroy - Meyers through the car window, shouting to reassure the locals: ' It's alright - don't worry'. In vain. Now in the back of the limo and struggling to make himself heard as it speeds off towards the main road out of town. In the distance police cars can be heard in pursuit -- by the sound of things they've just taken a wrong turning.

Lee Elroy - Meyers: ' Now then Maam I'm truly sorry to have inconvenienced you, but we do need your help. And of course we'll pay handsomely for your favours'

'What?!' Screams Mrs Wright. Elderly and outraged. ' How DARE you! I was brought up a good Methodist! If you think I am doing anything personal for you, you pig, you've got another think coming'. She tries hitting him again with her umbrella but the car restricts her movements. The driver tries to squirm out of the way as some of blows hit him. The car swerves all over the road. A double decker bus swerves out of the way. Meyers, desperately defending himself in the front passenger seat from the blows raining down on his right shoulder and neck. 'You've got it all wrong! I keep telling you - we only want to get you out to the farm.... '

Coming from a family whose relatives had been in some of the hardest fighting during the two world wars, Mrs Wright carries on hitting out and poking with her umbrella. The man in the back, all that is left of the three that got out originally in the high street is trying to stop her but getting nowhere. Her blows are telling. Meyers has blood coming from two cuts on the back of his head where the umbrella has done its work and he's bent down in the knee well holding himself and groaning. The car is hurtling down the country lanes with police cars in hot pursuit. Sirens wailing, blue lights flashing. Appearing and disappearing as the lane twists and turns.

Mrs Wright shouting: ' Yes and I know what happens to woman when thugs get them out to lonely farms. I've read all about it in the papers.

'Too I.D. your half brother Mrs Wright - nothing more. There's a thousand dollars in it for you if you'll help us' shouts Meyer still trying to get away from the very sharp pointed end of the umbrella.

Mrs Wright:: 'A thousand dollars! You didn't mention money before –

'We're here!' - this from the driver.

Meyers: 'You didn't give me a chance to mention it. What the...??..'

The American car has plunged down into a deep dell where the farm is located. Thick mist. Descending in layers.

Mrs Wright in a remarkable change of mood: 'It happens round here - something to do with the hills and the valleys. Come on, get your money bag out or whatever you carry to bribe people with.

At the farmyard the car doors open and the whole group gets out. Cold dank mist, and slurry type mud underfoot. They grope around trying to make sense of where they are. Neither the Americans or Mrs Wright are pleased about it. Lee Elroy - Meyers: ' Arrived in a storm and now this? Is this what this country is about? Thick mud, filthy weather and now fog??'

Mrs Wright: ' We didn't ask you here. And *I* didn't want to be here – remember....now where's the money' (staring hard at Meyers).

The party grope their way through the fog to the farm door. Farmyard machinery noises going behind closed barn doors can be heard. Sundry whooshes, knocks, bangs and muted lowing of cows and snufflings of pigs. On the way they meet one of Fred Driver's less than friendly members of the latter specie. Large White as it was known, that is currently running round its pen aggressively and is only restrained by the bars. The pen itself located outside very near to the farmhouse door Fred Driver is watching them quizzically from the doorway itself. He is in old corduroy trousers and old jumper and boots that look as though they date from the Second World War. When they we're washed by the look of it. Unlit Pipe hanging out the side of his mouth.

'Come to visit my pigs and cows is it? - don't worry about Hilda. She acts as guard dog'.

Lee Elroy - Meyers: 'Guard dog? It's a pig!?'

Fred Driver: ' Hilda's got a warped sense of humour. Had about 6 litters in her time. Her just acts as my guard dog, as I say. Well - can't call her a guard _pig_ can I!?' Meyers tiring of the conversation and wanting to get to the purpose of his visit 'Ok Ok, can we go inside do you think?'

Fred Driver: ' Being cleaned at the moment. Have to go inta cow barn'.

Cows being something of a sideline to the large pig pens. There's only so much you can take of pigs. Cows we're a distraction. Something that his uninvited guest Lee Elroy - Meyers was about to find out....

They enter a big milking parlour. Equipment clanking
away, cow noises and smells of cow. Sweet smells of dry
hay stored for winter feed, and sounds of heavy rain
hitting the tin roof above setting up noises like a hundred
kettle drums going at once. All of which gets right up
Meyers nose, in more ways than one. His London Savile
Row shoes and trousers are caked in wet mud and manure.
Meyers stands shivering with the foreboding that he has a
cold coming on...
They all stand around in a group near to the end of the line
of cows.
Constant interruptions in conversation caused by mooing
of cows and farm hands going too and fro in the
background monitoring the long line of milking
equipment. All the cows have names. The nearest one is
called Mirabel.

Several of the farmhands are working in and around the
cows with such comments as:
' There there, Mirabel, Sally, Jackie etc --- and what's
wrong with you today?'.
 Much patting and stroking of rumps and flanks to which
the cows respond flicking their tales and heads at their
handlers. Knowing who each one was.

However Mirabel, for some reason, did not take a liking
to Lee Elroy - Meyers, who oblivious to the cows mood
was approaching from the rear talking all the time to Fred
Driver about the tramp Henry and what had to be done to
find him. Mirabel looks round decides to lift her tail just

as Meyers his back turned to the cow is just raising his voice above the noise to make another point to Fred Driver. Faeces and thick liquid shoot out in a massive stream straight towards Meyers back. He of course is still wearing his caramel cream coloured suit complete with white Stetson.   Mirabel's accuracy had to be seen to be believed. The excrement hits Meyer in the upper back between the shoulder blades from the neck downwards. Lee Elroy - Meyers: ' Jesus, what the hell!! Get that damn cow away from me. I'm covered in shit!' Two other agents help to pull him away - trying to get his jacket off. Meyers: ' Jesus wept!   I come to this country and get rained on, mud and muck. Now a cow shits on my back. Mr Driver!? What else can happen?

Meyers standing there with excrement dripping down his back and trousers. One of his agents trying to shake off what he can from the jacket.

 'What sort of country is this for Christ sake!?'
Fred: 'Quite a lot still to come I'm thinking...' Referring more to the cow than the country.   Meyers storms out of the cow byre trying to throw off the rest of the muck from his back and legs...

Meyers misfortune has not gone unnoticed. Two Frenchman crouching behind a corner fence bordering the yard. Observing. They see Meyers stumbling out of the cow shed. Shouting and blaspheming. The French lough not understanding but glad to see the Americans not doing

very well. But they are about to have their own misfortune
on this foggy wet visit to Fred's farm.
One of the Frenchman is the Ist Secretary at the French
Embassy. His Excellency Etienne Flouru, a haughty man
with a low opinion of other embassy staff.
The other is the Head of Embassy security Mandel
Landers.

His Excellency: Can you see what is happening Mandel?
'The American Mr Meyers appears to be having an
argument with the farmer Mr Driver'.

'This is very awkward. We must not been seen to be
trespassing and the mud is sticking to my feet. You must
get closer Mandel! Ah - I will stay here''
Mandel: ' I think I can hear a little better your Excellency.
The American is asking the farmer what he knows about
the package'.
His Excellency: 'That is what we *all* wish to know! You
must get closer Mandel. It is *your* responsibility to find out
what has happened to *our property.*
Mandel: 'I know that your Excellency but....'
His Excellency looking over to the cow byre and frowning.
His family do not come from farming stock: 'Did not Mr
Meyers come in a white suit of some sort? Why is it now
black all down the back? What are they up too? Really! -
kneeling down here on all these bricks and in the mud ..!'
Shaking his leg fastidiously, his very expensive black
Embassy suit getting dirty. Trying to free himself from the

filth he has been kneeling in. Fred Drivers farm has never been known to be of the cleanest in Dorset....

Mandel referring to Meyers diplomatically: ' It would appear that a cow has raised it's tail to him your Excellency...'
 ' Really? That is interesting. Is it a local custom here in Dorset?'.
Neither of them see a large Alsatian (German Shepherd) dog approaching from behind. A proper guard dog this time, not like the pig Hilda stationed at the farms back door and looking fierce.

The dog has spotted the two intruders - the Frenchmen - crouching behind the wall where they clearly should not be. The dog is not used to seeing people crouching behind walls, fences or for that matter piles of bricks. Which in the Frenchman's case is clearly the situation. Neither would he know a French man from an Embassy anyway. They looked up to no good and being the guardian of the farm the dog decided to take action.

Assuming the aggressive posture for getting rid of intruders, the dog approaches, head down, fir bristling and mouth slavering. The animal, about the largest of its breed, creeps along the ground towards the two intruders. His Excellency Etienne Floure is just asking his Head of Security more questions, the latter saved from answering by what happens next. The dog leaps at His Excellency and sinks it's jaws into his elegant backside. .

His Excellency had been asking what there next move ought to be. His own next move is upwards as he let's out a scream of pain as the dogs teeth sink into his fleshy bottom.   Inside the barn the high pitched scream is heard by Fred Driver who thinks he has burglars. He runs for his shot gun. Shouting over his shoulder at the astonished Meyers and entourage: 'I think Toby has just found someone.... He rushes into a small hut and emerges carrying a wicked looking double barrelled shotgun. He is loading it with buckshot from his jacket pocket as he runs across the yard in the direction of the noise.

Etienne is still shouting fit to bust. Dancing around, his backside on fire.. .the dog is hanging on for grim death. Its whole jaw sunk into the Frenchman's backside.
' Get the dog off me' screams Etienne. 'Get it off!!' His whole face contorted in agony. Mandel. For the love of Christ'. Mandel leaps to one side, narrowly missing the dogs next attack as he releases one person and goes for the other. The dog steps back snarling at both of them. Fred arrives on the scene.

Fred: 'Back Toby! Good dog!   Good dog!'

Now then gentlemen perhaps you'd mind explaining yourselves'. Fred's voice is polite but the farmers shotgun is pointed at their chests and does not waver. The Americans are walking up behind to see the action.
His Excellency: 'For Gods sake call a doctor! I have been attacked by your dog Monsieur!.

Fred Driver - very cool: ' In due course Mr Eh...s?
Mandel Landers: This is His Excellency Etienne Floure,
First Secretary to the French Ambassador in London. Now
will you please call a doctor. His Excellency is *bleeding*.
Fred: You still haven't explained what or why you are on
my property, but come with me, my wife knows first aid.
Adding, she does a lot with the animals when the vet isn't
available. His Excellency is aghast. Hideous nightmare.
Oh why had he not stayed in London?   The whole episode
is watched with amusement by the Americans who keep
well out of the way. The French are led away, still at gun
point and the Americans discuss the matter.

Lee Elroy - Meyers: ' Seems we we're followed - can't
very well go into the farmhouse and show ourselves
anymore to the French contingent..
Mrs Wright: 'Can I go now. And I shall report you people
to the police!'
Lee Elroy - Meyers: 'Your privilege M-a-a-m but I should
point out that we are working with the co-operation of
your British police in this matter....'.
Mrs Wright has had quite enough of this loony and his
goons in dark glasses. She hits Meyers with her handbag
and stumps off towards the American Car. Meyers
stumbles backwards and falls down again collecting yet
more ordure. ' Jesus! What is it with that woman!'
Ist agent: Are you going to report to Langley on the
Embassy car phone Sir? They'll want to know what's
happening.

Lee Elroy - Meyers is not so sure about talking to Langley. His performance is not likely to enhance his reputation at CIA headquarters, let alone when *they* talk to the White House after his call. As for the President.......Best not to think about that or the type of people who might come knocking at his house in the small hours of the morning when he gets back.

'We're going to find that secret device if it's the last thing we do. No one calls me *The Big One* at Langley for nothing. I'm going to find that device or die in the attempt. Agent: ' Yes Sir...'   The agents look at each other. Meyers is known at Langley by a lot of other names other than "the Big One". Mainly to do with his inept handling of staff transfers and the like when in Personnel. People ending up in the oddest places unsuited to their abilities at the time.

They all get in the car and join an extremely fed up Eleanore Wright who completely avoids talking to anybody and has to be restrained from hitting Meyers again as he sits in the front stinking the car out after his experiences on the farm. This despite being cleaned up somewhat in the farm house.   They drive off back to Swingle Matravers and then to the Grosvenor Hotel in Swanage to recuperate..

The Bharunian contingent.

It is night time at the Drunken Cow public house and the Bharunian contingent are gathered in secret to discuss progress. Having been finally let go by the police with a caution about disturbing the peace. At either end of an upper floor there are two communal meeting rooms at opposite ends of the corridor. The Bharunians at one end and the Committee for Wealth in the other.

In the Bharunian meeting Prince Okamba is, once again, and predictably, bearing down on Sulu Wasei. This being the only way he can conceal his own failings.

'Well Sulu, what have you got to say for yourself? Where is the device?

Sulu: 'The villagers must have it'

Prince Okamba: 'Brilliant! You think I don't know that?'

Sulu Wasei: 'I do not think the French or the British have it. The Americans clearly don't and the South Africans who are around somewhere, don't appear to have it either. Else they would not all still be looking for our property.

Outside the window there is a flash of lightning and thunder. The Bharunian contingent cross themselves. Voodoo is in the air....

Prince Okamba raising his arms and looking upwards: 'It is a sign from God Sulu Wasei a <u>sign</u> from God! You must find the device within the next 24 hours. I give you 24 hours or your head will be on the block!

Sulu Wasei: ' Yes your Highness'.

At the other end of the corridor Fred Driver is chairing the Swingle meeting. The room is in semi darkness, only the main members, the inner circle, of the 'Committee for

Wealth' are present. These are: Fred Driver and his wife Jane. Bill Hutchings, John Hobson, Ian Samways and Linda Dodswell.
Fred: We've got to get the device out of the village to a safe hiding place'.
Linda: ' That's what your pig farm was supposed to be.'
Fred: ' Not since half the International Community started turning up?!
Possibly the high street? The others lean forward as Fred starts to explain.

Meanwhile down the other end of the narrow corridor in the Bharunian meeting room a local boy in the pay of the Bharunians is acting as messenger.
Boy: ' Do you know some of the villagers are meeting at the other end? I can hear them through the door.

Prince Okamba eyeing up this urchin: ' Keep your voice down, the public bar is near.. - go and find out what they saying'. He waves impatiently at the boy who disappears out of the room. Reaching the other end of the corridor he puts his ear to the door. Unfortunately for him at that end of the corridor the flooring right next to the door is uncarpeted. The badly fitting floorboards move and creak slightly when you stand on them. The door flies opens and John Hobson the Butcher towers over the urchin.
Grabbing him by the scruff of the neck before he can run, he drags the boy into the room.

John: ' Look what I found lurking outside the door. An eves dropper...' The boy is struggling and wriggling about like an eel.
Linda: ' It's Billy Samson isn't it. What are you doing?' .
Billy: ' Nothing miss - honest'.
John Hobson takes a swipe at the boy who wriggles away trying to get out of reach.
Linda: ' Your whole family spend their lives in trouble. So what are you doing in a public house might I ask??'.
Still dangling from John Hobson's long hairy forearm - unable to escape.
' The other lot want to know what your doing'.
Linda Dodswell: ' And paying you well for it I suppose? A word with your Headmaster in the morning my lad. ...'.
Billy turns white at the thought of seeing his school Headmaster, a tall gaunt elderly unsmiling man whose black suit hangs off his bony body. He likes to wield a lath strap and beat pupils.

Edmund Zachariah Johnson for that was his name, was a man who had been born and brought up in the Black Country town of Walsall with its factory chimneys and choking fumes from the many iron works in the area. Mr Johnson, or "old gruesome" as the school children called him behind his back, trained as a school teacher at Wakefield College, West Yorkshire and had gone to work at a small private school in his home town of Walsall where he had been for three years before being ejected for using excessive punishment. Just could not get the fact that corporal punishment had been banned and that parents

we're suing the school. Moving to Dorset some idiot in
the Education service had thought him suitable for a
primary school at Swingle. Doubtless thinking that
Swingle could do with some corporal punishment to bring
the unruly school children to heal. The official making
the decision had retired to North Wales without the benefit
of a leaving present or much else beyond the legal
minimum payment. Good riddance to him as far as his
colleagues we're concerned. Given all the complaints that
parents had been sending in about the school in Swingle
since the new teacher had come amongst them.

John who is still holding the wriggling squirming boy
takes a swipe at him. The boy trying to avoid the blows
raining down.
Linda: 'Your whole family spend their lives in trouble. So
what are you doing in a public house late evening might I
ask? I've asked you once already' Billy, still dangling
from John's long hairy forearm - unable to escape.
' The other lot want to know what your doing'.
Linda: ' I bet they are!   And paying you for it I suppose?
A word with your Headmaster in the morning my lad. I
know him well....'.   Billy turns even whiter than before at
the thought of seeing his school head teacher.
Billy: ' I'll do what you want'.
John Hobson: 'Very glad to hear it, now this is what I want
you to do. Go back to the Bharunian lot and tell them
you've been listening in and how we don't know anything.
We're in the dark about everything to do with the device
their looking for'.

Billy: 'Will they believe me? They've been going round everywhere trying to find it'. John hisses in the boys ear. 'We know that. And you'll know it if you don't convince them your genuine' .

Billy is dropped on the floor, picks himself up and runs for his life out of the door. Down the corridor and crashing straight into the Bharunians meeting room causing the big security man behind the door to take a swipe at him. Missing by a mile as the boy ducks away from the big meaty hand. They all stare at him. This nothing that is expendable.

Sulu Wasei: ' Well. What do they know?'

Billy: 'They don't know nothing'.

Prince Okamba: 'Really - are you speaking the truth?'

Billy: ' On my life I am.'

Prince Okamba stares at the boy. ' Yes'.

CHAPTER EIGHT
THE AMERICAN EMBASSY

The American Ambassador to London, Mr Maynard, is in conference with Lee Elroy - Meyers, who has been called back overnight from Dorset to report.

The Ambassador exasperated: 'So you don't know where this device is?'

Meyers: ' We've searched that village and can't find any trace of it. We've even been out to the farm where the head honcho of the village's: 'Committee for Wealth' Fred

Driver lives. He doesn't know either. So he says anyways'.
The Ambassador:: ' I heard about it. The French ended up in the mud?'
Meyers suddenly getting het up, not a thing to do in the Ambassador's inner office or sanctum:
'I think we should swamp the place with people. Saturate it.
Shouting red faced: Nuke the village!'. (The irony of his own words is lost on him).
A side door opens in the wood panelling, a man stands in the doorway. 'Alright Ambassador?' Undoubtably one of the security contingent at the embassy. Obviously they heard the raised voice of Meyers.   'Yes I'm fine, I'm fine thank you'.   The man withdraws, not before giving Meyers a look clearly warning him to keep is voice down and remember where he is.

The Ambassador continues - very quietly: 'This is England not Vietnam Mr Meyers. Looking at his watch. 'I'm due a Reception at Buckingham Palace - I don't think the British, let alone Her Majesty the Queen , will like us destroying an English village'.
 Meyers: 'No Sir'.
The Ambassador as an afterthought whilst moving round his desk: 'Have you tried searching from the air? Or going underground?' '
This turns out to be a very unfortunate comment. Meyers is a very literal sort of person.

'Going underground Sir? You mean using a mole device in a tunnel?
The Ambassador: ' Are there tunnels at Swingle Matravers ?
 Meyers: ' There's an ancient castle called "Corfe Castle" which has tunnels Sir, it could be in one of them. Could be - if we can't get this device then no one else will'.
The Ambassador: ' Blow up the tunnels you mean? No, for the same reasons I gave before.
Besides I've been to Corfe Castle, it's a big place with a lot of history. My daughter went walking there at Durlston country park over to Worth Matravers only a month ago with some friends from her College she goes to over here. Educational trip staying locally down there for the week. Search the tunnels Mr Meyers by all means, those that are accessible; but don't blow them up!'
' Yes Sir!!': Lee Elroy - Meyers in his best ex Marines voice, back ramrod stiff , saluting the Ambassador.
The Ambassador sighs inwardly, clearly wondering why Washington landed him with this nut. Such a delicate job. A sledgehammer to crack a nut. Is that what the British say? He sighs again, only inwardly this time. Looking wonderingly at this clown standing in front of him. Langley must have been desperate to get rid of him.
The Ambassador: ' You have about 5 days to find the device. Our intelligence suggest the village people will try to sell to the highest bidder'.
Lee Elroy - Meyers - eyes lit up and snapping his fingers: ' I could subject all the villagers to a lie detector test Mr Ambassador'.

The Ambassador stares very hard at this man Washington have sent over. Standing there in his flamboyant clothing like something out of a Clint Eastwood Spaghetti Western film. Holding an enormous white Stetson hat.

'This is England Mr Meyers not America or some third world hick country. They won't stand for it!'. Almost adding but restraining himself, a remark that he might get shut on like he was by that cow in Fred Driver's cow shed. His secret service report on what had been going on with Meyers and the South Africans and French in Dorset, had been very thorough. It had made incredible reading. The Ambassador had almost dropped his coffee cup whilst reading it.

Meyers: 'Then what 'll I do?'.

The Ambassador , exasperated: ' I don't care what you do! But you have the authority of the President of the United States to find that device and bring it back to America. Just don't upset the Brits!   Adding patiently as though speaking to a very small child:

'The Bharunians stole it from the French in the first place, and therefore have no right to it anyway. The French want it back but they are not going to get it. You are here Mr Meyers to bring it back to America. Do you see now?'

Meyers showing no sign that he has heard the Ambassador. ' I've decided to take up your suggestion of Aerial surveillance Sir'.

' My suggestion!? Keep me out of it!'.

Meyers: ' A hot air balloon gala Sir. The villagers are
having a village fete soon - with balloons in a nearby field.
Perfect cover to go over the countryside - over peoples
houses and farms. See if we spot anything.
The Ambassador: ' A hot air balloon? Loaded with secret
agents?
You are suggesting that the US government fly over the
British countryside and in British air space in some kind of
blacked out stealth balloon?!'
Meyers: ' Yes Sirree Sir!   As I say Sir. The villagers
have this fete which includes hot air balloons. What's one
more balloon amongst so many? Perfect cover.
The Ambassador with his last shred of patience: ' Do it but
don't bring me or the American Embassy into it. But
whatever happens find that device - the US government
can use it to make billions on the stock market and we
need it; if that device is hooked up to our computers'. We
could use the money to help pay off the national debt, or
part of it anyway.

' You bet Sir'. At a nod from the Ambassador Meyers
turns and marches smartly from the room.

The Ambassador, soberly suited for Buckingham Palace,
his silver grey hair carefully groomed, stands behind his
desk watching him go, a creepy dread feeling seeming to
crawl up his spine as he stands there. He wonders if it
might be time for another posting. Or maybe just to tell
Mildred, his wife, to pack their bags and head back to
Minnesota; sending in an overdue request for a vacation .

Trouble is, he has only recently arrived in the UK ten months ago....what the *hell* had Washington been thinking about with this person!....he'd heard of the man of course, at least what they had on Background, which was not very much.
Perhaps they could post Meyers to some remote place in Arkansas.   Best place for him in the Ambassadors opinion. He sat down heavily, pressing the bell on his desk for coffee. Maybe he should start asking for tea as a way of blending in.....?
All the young suited assistant saw when he opened the door to the Ambassadors room in answer to the summons, was to see his tall very distinguished looking Ambassador slumped groaning with his head in his hands....
London was turning out to be an interesting first posting the young man thought. Something to tell his parents in Cincinnati about next time he wrote........ Funny place, London... the girls we're nice though, hmmm....... The young man quietly withdrew to get more coffee. Looked as though the Ambassador needed it....perhaps with an extra shot of Espresso....

South African Embassy.

The South African Ambassador His Excellency Mr Ngobizitha Gugu Chisomo was a big imposing man with a big imposing voice. Dressed in a rich dark blue pinstripe suit as befitted his corporate lawyers background before he got asked by the South African government to come into their service.

'So despite having ten of our very best agents you can't find this secret stock market forecasting device? You've asked everywhere?'

Yannis Nour: ' I've managed to learn from our Intelligence service that the device gives off a lot of heat when it's activated'.

The Ambassador: ' So? - what do you propose?'

Yannis Nour: 'Use a helicopter with a heat seeking device. We've got one of ours over here now; fitted with new avionics by the British that needs test flying - perfect cover. We fly it over Dorset. Anybody asks - we're just testing it out and the British Government know about it since they sold us the software package and that it has fitted into our helicopter. It's already in the south of England awaiting these tests.

The Ambassador: ' Then do it!. Get on with it. We haven't much time'.

Meanwhile back at the Bharunian camp which has now moved to a cramped back street house in Swingle (they never seem to get it right!) Prince Okamba is addressing his group of jaded followers. Those who are not out searching for Henry the tramp that is, and the parcel or bag containing the device. The Prince has something important to tell us:

' Our Embassy in London has had a fax from His Majesty, my older brother, heaven bless him, King Obanda the 3rd who has decreed that we must find the device by Saturday.

That is five days time! Or I have to return and face him.
And you (!) Sulu Wasei, arm flung out, finger pointing,
will have to return with me as well'.

The room is deathly quiet. They all know what it means.
The firing squad for Sulu Wasei and for most of them as
well. In fact a bullet in the chest would be the least of their
worries compared with what would have been going on in
the cells, days before they we're, eventually, dragged, feet
first, out to the execution posts in the middle of the market
square. Those, that is, that had not been killed by any
poisonous snakes that somehow had got into the cells
earlier in their detention. When they we're sleeping.

What was that expression? "Dead men walking?".
Would just about describe it for most of them; furtively
looking at each other around the room.
Sulu Wasei however appears untroubled by the situation.
He was a good actor.

Sulu: ' The villagers have a fete on and I think they will
use this event to get rid of the device. I hear the Americans
are going to search for it from the air. So *we* will look both
on the ground *and* in the air - the Americans must not beat
us'. Much emphatic nodding and affirmative mutterings
around the room.
Prince Okamba, his voice silky with menace and looking
straight at Sulu Wasei through slitted snakes eyes:
'And how exactly do you propose to do this Sulu?'

Sulu: 'By posing as visitors from a charity and running a stall at the fete. We can run a fortune telling tent'. Sulu Wasei holds his arms up theatrically. His hands arms and face raised as if in supplication to the Gods:
' Ancient wisdom from Africa - Palm Reading a speciality'.

 "Trite" would be the word to describe this performance.

Prince Okamba coldly: 'Very impressive. They had better believe you SULU WASEI. You are running out of lives. Right now a cat would have more lives that you possess'.

Sulu continues: - 'And in the air we will have a radio controlled model aeroplane with camera slung beneath with weapon pods. One of your entourage has been learning to use it'. 'Our technical section could adapt the plane' The technical section, comprising three young people whose so called technical experience had been gained in a local evening class tinkering with radio and television sets. They look on apprehensively. Press ganged into helping out with the model plane when they had actually all been grouped around an ancient toaster in the "fully equipped modern kitchen" which this rented terraced house at the back of Swingle was supposed to have. The toaster had been the only source of warmth in the kitchen. The 'fully equipped bit' came from the short term rental contract that had been signed by their bosses the previous day with the owner. He himself had been passing in a pick up truck which happened to be loaded

with a lot of dead carcasses. Reminding all of them
ominously of Oshasha, when the prison was having a clear
out. Only in that case it was dead humans not animals that
we're being cleared out. Feet and legs hanging out the
back of the truck... rather like the carcases they had seen
yesterday.
 'I hope for your sake it works. I've never heard of such a
situation' said Prince Okamba doubtfully.
Sulu Wasei: 'We purchased the plane this morning and
fitted the small surveillance camera to it..' Pulling away a
cover from an object previously hidden on a large side
table as he says this. Underneath is a 3 foot long silver
coloured propeller driven American P 51 Mustang A
fighter plane from the second world war. Underneath it the
thin oblong shape can be seen. This is the aerial camera.

Sulu Wasei continuing: ' - the pictures beamed back to a
small television screen in the Embassy car. If it sees
anything suspicious we will know'. Those around Sulu are
impressed. For once even Prince Okamba is silent.

CHAPTER NINE
THE VILLAGE FETE

In a field on the edge of Swingle Matravers. The field is a
riot of colour. Marquees, village stalls selling home
produce. Fairground.

A mass of village people and tourists milling around the stalls enjoying themselves. Judging from the numbers of people at the stalls the fete is big success.

In the middle of the mass of stalls the Bharunians have set up their fortune tellers tent with a painted sign telling people that a genuine African Witch Doctor is giving advice about the future. A number of curious onlookers already beginning to form a queue.
Further over in the field the Americans are manning a covert operation from behind the 'Bring and Buy' stall selling raffle tickets to aid the one hundred year old *Wishing Well* installed last year by the Swingle Matravers 'Committee for Wealth'.

Not too far away the South Africans at their table have erected a 6 foot high model of Table Mountain, plus a model of the village where President Nelson Mandela lived. A hastily arranged history lecture concerning the life and times of this famous man is being delivered by a member of the Embassy education section who has come down overnight. A side stall selling miniature versions of the South African flag and copies of a childrens picture book of the country normally presented to school children who visit the embassy with their teachers on a school trip. The books also brought down by the education officer in his car.

Hot Air Balloons.

In a nearby field a brilliant display of multi coloured many hued balloons are being prepared and sent aloft one by one at the direction of the marshals in charge. The marshals talking to each other and their control centre set up in a tent on the edge of the ground. Talking to the Balloon pilots telling them the take off sequence for the balloons, wind conditions and any other matters they need to know about.

Balloons of all shapes and sizes depicting Castles, Country Houses, Cars, Noahs Arks, Busses and Lorries and even Bananas and assorted baskets of fruit. All showing off the balloon manufacturers pop art to good effect . Reds, Greens, Purples, Yellows and Blue. Stripes, Verticals, Diamonds and wavy lines. A visual kaleidoscope of rainbow colours to delight and dazzle the eye.
Gas jet blowers being prepared and tested. Roaring away as the balloons prepare for lift off. Straining against the ground ropes. The balloon minders looking towards the marshals awaiting the signal to release mooring lines. Much crackling of radios and tinny voices of people coming through from other parts of the ground.

The American balloon is already up, high above the field; a large canary yellow   banana with the basket hanging beneath. Lee Elroy - Meyers and two of his security people are in the basket with the pilot and his assistant. The camera is equipped with sophisticated infra red and vibration detectors tuned to pick up the slightest vibrations or heat from the hidden stock market device on the ground now far below. A large rather lopsided Antenna array strapped onto the side and corner of the basket pointing downwards. Its sensors have their work cut out trying to separate out the Device they are seeking on the ground from all the other heat sources around. Namely heat given off from all the domestic kitchen appliances in peoples houses. Especially as due to delays with the weather it is now near lunchtime and those not at the fair are cooking in the houses below.

Several other hot air balloons are getting very close to the American balloon. The pilot already juggling with the imbalance to the basket caused by the large aerial array mounted to one side of the basket. Also trying to avoid the other balloons most of whom appear to be much larger than their own.
A large country house is currently floating past followed by a vintage Rolls Royce. Followed by a garden shed.

To say that Lee Elroy - Meyers is not a happy man would be an understatement.
Not helped by the fact that it is very hot, their own balloon a giant yellow banana, all they could get at short notice looks stupid - and the technical people can't get the camera working properly that they brought down overnight from London.

Lee Elroy - Meyers testily: ' I thought you guys we're experts!?'
 Sergeant Johnson: ' It's the atmospheric conditions Sir. The balloons heat is affecting the camera. Don't forget it's infra red sir. Not to mention all these other balloons going past... looking across as he says this at a lot of people in a basket slung under the Country House and who are drinking champaign served by someone dressed as a Butler. Raising their glasses of bubbly and laughing fit to bust at the big yellow Banana that Meyers and his crew are using...

Lee Elroy - Meyers: 'The pilots got to fly the thing dammit'.
Sergeant Johnson: 'We're trying Sir'.
Suddenly there goes buzzing and zooming past the balloon a silver coloured model aeroplane just missing the balloon. Meyers: ' What the hell!'. Consternation.
 ' Jesus! What was that!'. Meyers hanging on for dear life.
'I don't know!'.
' It's coming again. Lose height, lose height!' one of the agents yelling at the pilot, a local man commissioned to do the flight. The model plane is flying about banking and weaving around the Americans. The pilot frantically pulls the rip cord to let gas out of the balloon. The cord is jammed. The model plane coming in again as if to attack the basket and all it contents, namely Meyers. The occupants ducking to avoid the plane. As the plane goes past it launches a small red flare from the pod attached to

the wings. It is aimed straight at the basket. It hits the
basket and flames leap up . Panic ensues with the pilot and
his assistant reaching for the fire extinguishers. The
balloon rocking crazily from side to side as people
stampede about in the basket.
On the ground Sulu Wasei is operating the model plane.
'Did we get the balloon?' Another with the binoculars
trained on the balloon above: ' It's on fire. No wait! - it hit
the basket. There trying to put it out'.
In the balloon foam is being poured foam onto the fire
inside one corner of the basket. The fire, which is actually
only in one small corner of the balloon and caused by the
red flare hitting an old newspaper discarded in the corner,
is doused. The balloon is bucking madly - see sawing this
way this way and that. Meyers, like everybody else
hanging on for dear life, some of his team are being sick
over the side. He grabs a gun from the bottom of his bag
and putting it on automatic fires a spray of bullets in a
wide arc at the model plane which is turning in a tight
circle and coming back. The bullets miss the model plane
and hit another balloon that is tracking across left to right
immediately behind the model plane. The occupants of the
other balloon basket slung under what looks like a
traditional canal narrow boat look alarmed as with a loud
hissing they start to go down. Jettisoning water ballast to
try and slow their descent.
'Sir!'
' I know - missed dammit' Meyers said.
The pilot of the canal boat is urgently trying to pull the rip
cord to reduce height and find a safe landing area.

Technical Sergeant Johnson: ' The cameras working again'
.
The operator starts to scan the ground by using the small screen inside a knap sack as order out of chaos is restored to the balloon and the smoke from the flare disappears. But Lee Elroy - Meyers blood is up. He is fighting mad at the Bharunians – 'Look its coming back!' . The model plane zooms past and Meyers taking aim fires several more rounds at it and manages to hit the tail section. The model flies on and away yawing first one way then the other. Meyers: 'It's still going.   Look out!'.
The pilot distracted by all this has run into another balloon shaped like the British Lion. The Lion and the Banana look as though they are locked together in their death throes. Wires and trailing mooring lines become entangled. Balloons everywhere start taking avoiding action. A melee of balloons going up, down, sideways. Swooping behind other balloons with much blowing of gas jets and people waving their arms about. The marshals on the ground speaking through loud speakers from the ground. Trying to get the pilots attention and telling them to land.

More pandemonium in the air as the model aircraft flies round seemingly desperate to get away from the maze of balloons. Red dye streaking out from behind the plane. On the ground Bharunians are gathered around Sulu Wasei who has wrenched the controls from the young operator and is himself trying to control the plane. Desperate conversations ensue as everybody tries to offer advice. The police are fast approaching the stall.

In the air more balloons collide with each other and the baskets get entangled. Desperate mid air dance of balloons trying to get away from each other. Suddenly a flare is fired from the ground to a point high above where the balloons are. The emergency signal from the ground Marshall cancelling the display and ordering people to land. Radios crackling in the balloons as the Marshall's instructions are reinforced by his assistants on the ground shouting through loudspeakers. The model aeroplane finally emerges and heads for the ground.

The police start talking to the Bharunians. Police radios going off everywhere. There are four of them looking hard at the Bharunians and demanding explanations. Another group are going through the crowds taking statements. Ambulances are arriving at the other end of the field near the emergency exit to take away anybody who needs hospital treatment from the mid air collisions.

' What's going on! What do you think your doing? Can't you control it?' Sulu Wasei mutters something in his local village dialect that no one understands.

The policeman, an athletic type lunges for the radio control panel of the model aircraft. Sulu Wasei backs off refusing to hand over the control. The police lunge at him again. There is a struggle.

'Look!!' - a villager staring, arm and finger pointed upward.

The model plane is coming straight for the tent the Witch Doctor is using for fortune telling. Feet away from where they are standing. It screams to earth , a flaming torch crashing straight into the tent. Screaming. People running everywhere. A local reserve fire crew had been carrying out demonstrations with the turntable ladder – now they are fighting a real fire. The model plane, an incendiary device now in all but name has crashed onto the table the Witch Doctor has been using upsetting bowls of coloured fluids and effigies and fetishes used as props for his forecasting have fire. Straw bales, bone dry and meant for the donkeys elsewhere in the field are stacked too near to the table. They are smouldering as well. Flames coming from the nearest bale.

Above all this the balloons are moving away. Giving themselves space to land individually. Balloons are starting to come down mainly in nearby farmers fields flattening whatever crop is being grown.

Lee Elroy - Meyers, still aloft, is huddled in the corner of the American Balloon.
'Get this dang thing on the ground. I want to see what's going on down there.

Technical Sergeant Johnson: ' What about the infra red?'.
Lee Elroy - Meyers: 'Who cares! with a fire like that going on? You think you would pick up anything? Two of the stalls are in flames'.
On the ground the Witches tent, the table and the straw bales are now all engulfed in flames. Too near to the other stalls, the nearest of which is going up in flames also. The witch doctor is seen fleeing from the tent his ornamental

cloak on fire. Not to mention what looks like a wig he is wearing with a high back to it.

The fire brigade are frantically trying to stem the fires. Two of their members running after the witch doctor with a fire extinguisher. Calling for reinforcements. The police are moving people away down to the other end of the field. A loud Hailar in use . At the far end an ambulance is making its way out of the field, its lights flashing. Not everybody queuing outside the fortune tellers tent have got away unscathed. The police are telling people to keep calm. Directing them to the other end where the refreshment marquee is located near the entrance. The vicar, the Reverend West alerted by all the noise and mayhem has come across from the church with his wife plus other helpers to see what they can do to help.

The fire is being brought under control and the fete continues up the other end of the field, with the Vicar being prevailed upon to announce the next event. This is a parachute drop by a local club. All the balloons now having landed or about to land.

In the distance a light plane approaches and out of it came four parachutists. These 'daredevils of the sky' have a perfect view of the ground. A radio crackles telling the parachutists to head for a field opposite the fete. This is acknowledged.

On the ground the police are talking to the Bharunians who all seem to be claiming diplomatic status and immunity from prosecution.

The police back off for consultations - but still keep a wary eye.

The South Africans, French and the British are all conferring. Allies in adversity, it is the first time that all three parties have come together and acknowledged each others existence since being in Dorset for a week and a half. Gloating over the Bharunians misfortune.

His Excellency Etienne Floure: 'It would seem gentlemen that the Bharunians latest escapade has ended in ruins, and not for the first time'.

Yannis Nour: ' Sure. Anybody else find the device yet? Not us. The only success we've had was our model of Table Mountain'. Looking ruefully at the smouldering remains of the model amongst the ruins of the stalls following the fire.

Sydney Thomson - Jones importantly: ' Well - on behalf of Her Majesties Government I can say that our researches our continuing'.

His Excellency Etienne Floure (in jocular vain): 'So the British have not found it either - and in your own country!' Looking at the others in a superior manner. – ' Do we believe the British when they say that they have not found it?? Should we ever believe the British?'

Sydney Thomson - Jones, looking at the Frenchman and thinking that the one hundred year long war with the French is justified if this pompous idiot is a true example of that countries so called aristocratic classes.

' You may believe what you like Sir. If we had found it we would hardly be standing here in a field in Dorset talking to you .

His Excellency Etienne Floure: 'My dear Sydney - I am only playing with your emotions'.   The senior British official scowls ....

Yannis Nour: ' But where do we go from here? The device has *got* to be around here somewhere'.

His Excellency is saved from replying by the village band starting up a strident tune. The fete, despite everything, is still continuing. A panoply of coloured tents, people milling around the remaining stalls and having a go on the dodgems, helter skelter, hall of mirrors, coconut shy, shooting range, guess the weight and assorted hoopla stalls with their stuffed teddy bears as prizes.   The villages bric a brac and catering stalls with tea urn and rock cakes and cheese sandwiches on sale are starting to gear up again. The smouldering remains of the witch doctors tent and nearby tables being taped off. .

Meanwhile in a cottage in the High Street of Swingle Matravers, Linda Dodswell sits in her kitchen looking at a brown paper parcel. Linda is sipping tea. A contented smile on her face.

Inside the bag a small red light can be seen winking on and off. The stock market forecasting device. It has been entrusted to Linda for the afternoon by the other members of the Committee for Wealth.

The fair goes on well into late evening. The crowds disperse, eventually leaving the organizers to clear up the field. The balloon enthusiasts having packed up and long gone. Some of their number have been carted off to

hospital and the walking wounded allowed to go home.
Teams of people comprising the ground support with their
Land Rovers and trailers are packing up the balloons.   The
various security groups have retreated to their hotels and
guest house accommodation. Leaving the fire brigade and
the police to compare notes and then move off themselves.
A security firm now manning the gate to make sure no one
walks off with any equipment left in the field overnight.

Conference by the Bharunians:

The following morning in Sulu Wasei's bedroom at the run
down rented back street house now serving as a temporary
extension to their London Embassy. Trying to be
inconspicuous. Hopeless as they could not have broadcast
their presence more fully if they had gone around in a
procession with multicoloured banners. The whole
Bharunian group walking around and intimidating the
villagers for days on end, resulting in numerous complaints
to the police about their behaviour.   Not to mention what
had happened on the floor of the Butchers shop when
they'd tried to interrogate John Hobson the Butcher!
Leaving one dead and another injured. It was a miracle
they had not all been deported. Let alone still allowed to be
in Dorset.
As a result numbers of the original Embassy staff we're
now helping police with their enquiries. This included the
heavy who had interrogated the driver in the basement.
So at least the driver who was still part of the contingent

did not have him to worry about! For the time being anyway.

Prince Okamba glowering over everybody in the room.
Sulu Wasei: ' The model plane episode was unfortunate....
Prince Okamba: ' Yes - the witch doctor will never be the same again'. Showing an unusual sense of humour. ' But as it was one of my village in laws that got singed by the flames I am not that bothered'. Laughter..
Sulu Wasei taking advantage of this rare moment of good humour to ask:
' I was just about to say your Excellency that if the device is not above ground then it might be below....'
Prince Okamba: ' What do you mean?'
Sulu Wasei has an old map of the area. Obtained from a second hand book shop half way down Swanage High Street.
Prince Okamba: Did you steal that map? I hear the museum at Wareham got broken into'. Jocular laughter...
Sulu Wasei: 'The police are searching but why should they suspect us, I bought this from a shop in Swanage'.
Prince Okamba: ' You are either very naive or very stupid Sulu Wasei - after what happened at the fete. Buying maps I mean. *We* are the ones confined to our bedrooms by the local police - not the Americans. British, French or South Africans.
Sulu Wasei: ' I have another idea'.
Prince Okamba: ' Make it good Sulu Wasei. Make it good.
Sulu Wasei: 'We use the tunnels'.
Prince Okamba: ' The tunnels'.

Sulu Wasei: ' The tunnels'.

Prince Okamba stares at Sulu Wasei expressionless. He hasn't the faintest idea what tunnels Sulu Wasei is talking about. Neither, to be fair, had anybody else.

Sulu Wasei improvising like mad: 'These tunnels we're used by escaped prisoners from Corfe Castle in the Thirteenth Century'.

Prince Okamba: 'Really ? I had not heard of it. And you think we should look for the device down there? Why?'.

Sulu Wasei, still hastily improvising: 'At the village fete I overhead Mr Driver - the chairman of their so called ' Committee for Wealth' say that they would hide the device in a tunnel. The only tunnel around here is the one under Corfe Castle'.

Prince Okamba gets up from his armchair. His entourage shuffle around him to give room in the cramped space.

Prince Okamba: 'I am going to give you this one last chance Sulu Wasei. One last chance to redeem yourself ,otherwise I will take over completely and you my dear 'friend' will return post haste to Oshasha where you will explain yourself to His Majesty King Obanda the 3rd. And we both know what that means don't we? Both parties eye each other up. Sulu Wasei realizes that he has to get rid of Prince Okamba as well as the meddlesome package they are looking for, if he is to escape with his life and implement the next part of his plan.

Sulu is getting very fed up with Okamba's constant threats about Oshasha. One way or another Okamba has to be dealt with. But these thoughts he keeps to himself.

CHAPTER TEN.
CORFE CASTLE.

In a car outside the tunnel entrance some distance from the castle gatehouse.
A quarter moon casts deep shadows across the tall castellated remains of the ruined castle walls and moat, with the village beyond. Off to one side the Bharunians are clustered together preparing to enter a dank noisome tunnel entrance that has all the appearance (for good reason) of a large sewer pipe. Over to one side the British contingent is keeping an eye on things.

On the basis of British fair play and 'best man or woman win', they have not told the others that they had bugged the Bharunians rooms as soon they moved in and had been doing so ever since.   The Americans, in the same spirit of co-operation have not told their hosts the British, or the South Africans or the French for that matter that they too have found out about the tunnel the Bharunians are about to go down. The French and South Africans are wise to it.. They on principal have not been telling anybody anything outside their own four walls.
Everybody is hiding in different parts of the outer boundary area of the castle grounds without being spotted by the others. Each trying to keep a surreptitious eye on the other. The spirit of international co operation has never been greater. They are all determined to get to the device first, worth billions to the country, and stuff everybody else!

The village clock strikes Eleven.   It is very dark and the wind is getting up.

Sulu Wasei is assembled with his team. Prince Okamba: has condescended to come along and offer moral support. He needs to. Most of the remaining Bharunian team have had enough of the escapade to Dorset and want to go back to London. If not home, where they will disappear back to their villages in the bush. Those who are not planning to claim political asylum meantime.

The Tunnel entrance.

Sulu Wasei turning to Prince Okamba: ' Are you coming too Sir?
Prince Okamba: 'No - To you goes the honour'.
Sulu Wasei through gritted teeth - 'Thank you Your Highness'.
Sulu turns and faces the entrance to the tunnel. It is about 4 feet high and square facing with a door grill padlocked to the front. Out of nowhere Sulu Wasei produces a key.
Prince Okamba: 'I will not ask where the key came from Sulu Wasei. A friendly villager perhaps?'
Sula coldly: 'Since you do not wish to come with us – it is perhaps better that you do not know'.
Prince Okamba glares at Sulu Wasei but says nothing. He knows that Wasei is being tactful in front of the larger group; but that the gloves are now well and truly off.
Prince Okamba begins to wonder if he did the right thing with all those public threats - but it is all much too late

now. Everything is too late where this escapade in England is concerned.

The rough wooden door with its padlock opened, is now pulled back. Torches flash into the forbidding dripping darkness beyond. Drip, drip, drip.   The dank coldness of the tunnel seeping through the clothes of the Bharunian party. The tunnel stretching out in stygian blackness beyond. Rats scurrying away to who knew what that beyond.....

Hiding behind some fallen rocks from the Castle, the British contingent are watching the Bharunians enter the sewer pipe.

Sydney Thomson - Jones: ' Can they see us do you think?'

Military security: 'No Sir. We're quite hidden'.

Sydney: 'What <u>are </u>they doing?'

Security: 'I checked Sir, it's a very large diameter concrete drain pipe running underground half way up the slope towards the castle itself. A later edition. Not medieval. Part of a flood defence scheme the local council thought up just before the Second World War to stop the castle grounds getting so boggy. Used to be a quagmire apparently, round this side of the castle. Some local Borough Engineer type person at the time thought the scheme up. But it wasn't very successful. Got used as part of the local defences in the war. The pipe was abandoned later on. They'd thought up some other drainage schemes which proved more effective. But the <u>original</u> pipe was not removed and is still connected up.   Do we follow Sir?'

Sydney Thomson - Jones: ' Yes but wait a bit. We don't want to meet the Bharunians inside, let them get up the tunnel - -- now get your team ready'.   They prepare. Crouching down, faces blacked up, waiting for the order to go in.

Meanwhile from the other side of the road and towards the end of the street the American contingent are watching. It is starting to rain. A depressing Dorset misty drizzle. Meyers stands smoking a cigar: 'What the *hell* are they doing??' Meaning the Bharunians.
Sergeant Johnson with exaggerated patience, 'Going down the tunnel Sir'.
Lee Elroy - Meyers exasperated: ' I can see that dammit!
Technical Sergeant Johnson: 'Do we follow Sir?'.
Lee Elroy - Meyers: 'You bet your ass we follow. Where the B-h-a-r-h-r-u-n-I-a-n-s can go the United States can go. Have you got that Sergeant?
The sergeant salutes smartly. 'Yes Sir!'. Very loudly.
Meyers looking round: ' Shuddup for Christ sake! . You want everyone to hear?' 'You no what the time is?'.
Technical Sergeant Johnson: ' No Sir, sorry Sir'.
'Then get on with it!'. But in the dark Meyers in turning in the blackness backs up against the Sergeant who knocks the man behind him who steps sideways and backwards into several dustbins left outside a shop for the refuse lorry in the morning. One of the dustbin lids come off and clatters on the kerb stone, rolling down the road taken by the wind and banging into a car. More noise as the car alarm goes off with a high pitched wining sound.

In the tunnel entrance Sulu Wasei hears the noise:'What was that? ' the others further up the tunnel with its thick concrete walls turn and listen. Hearing nothing but what they take to be the wind the group moves further into the tunnel. They inch forward forgetting about Okamba. It is dead silent. Superstitious thoughts crowd in on the Bharunians. From out of nowhere comes a voice. ' Be quick!' Okamba shouting from the entrance, annoyed that the group had made so little progress. Everybody jumps. Sulu Wasei looks round alarmed at his boss shouting when everybody is trying not to be heard. He see's Okamba standing just outside the entrance, bending his body down to peer up the tunnel at them. The street lamp outlining his bulky frame.

Okamba in a hoarse whisper: ' The Americans are over by the hut opposite. They must have seen you. Be quick in your search. I will try and distract them'.

Bharunian whispering:'How will he do that?!' .

Sulu sotto voce: 'Put a curse on them probably – now come on before it's too late'.

The torches move forward. The tunnel is in stygian gloom. Drip, drip, drip of water coming down from the ceiling. The ground rough underfoot. Just to improve things further the place has been used as a dumping ground for old household rubbish. Rats scurrying hither and thither. Damp cold seeping through the Bharunians thin clothing, trainers and socks. Tramping along through nearly 100 yards of underground pipe. Dark, dank and not able to see much ahead. Rats skittering away under their feet. They

had just gone past the half way point when suddenly they start to hear noises behind them - far off and coming closer. Nearby there are other smaller flood tunnels leading off. The Bharunians are superstitious.
'What's that noise? Sounds like an animal!' Wasei: 'Quiet. Keep your torches on the ground. Listen!'
In the tunnel there is a silence except for constant dripping. Rats scurry past. Distant groaning noises. The tunnel is acting as an echo chamber for the trees above. Wind chasing through the branches of the trees. The sounds of footsteps get closer.
Sulu Wasei shouting in a hoarse whisper: ' Keep moving'
Keep moving! The eeriness of the place is getting to them; including him!

The party reluctantly move forward. Silence apart from the wind and the dripping noises. Cut off from the world. Blackness in front and no one looking behind for fear of what they might see. Suddenly up ahead and in a nearby feeder tunnel for the rain water. High pitched screeching noises. Hundreds and hundreds of tiny bats, hanging down from the top of the pipe where there is a railing running along. A thin conduit inside the railing. The bats have made it there home. Now they are being disturbed by all the noise of humans coming along with torches. The Bharunians freeze their actions, hoping the bats will settle down again. Eventually, after what seems an age, they do. Or seem to.

A long way back thin pin pricks of light from torches pointed towards the ground. The American party have started their journey up the tunnel. Creeping along, blacked up and wearing thick rubber soled boots.
Lee Elroy - Meyers - whispering - 'Did you hear anything?'
Sergeant Johnson: 'No Sir'.
The American party move forward with Lee Elroy - Meyers who has decided to join the group after all. Not least because they don't seem to be making much progress and it might look good on his report to the President and Langley back home. The Americans are finding the tunnel dank, creepy, full of dripping noises and sounds of rats scuttling across the rough uneven floor. No one wants to meet what maybe up ahead. Discord within the group, muttering: 'Is this tunnel haunted? – weird..'. Jesus, where are we.... Is the castle haunted...? Special forces should be doing this, not us....
Meyers: 'Keep moving - we gotta keep moving forward'. Reluctantly the party move on in the unrelieved gloom. Suddenly a flash as bright as day ahead, just as suddenly cuts off. 'What the hells that!'. --- 'Don't know'.
The party continue forward quickening their pace. But keeping well behind the leader Meyers. If there's anything ahead - he gets it first. Meyers is mystified. A few minutes ago he was at the back, but now he seemed to be at the front? How did that happen?

Back at the tunnel entrance the British party convene a hasty conference.

Sydney Thomson - Jones.: ' No point in our going in there.
Where does the tunnel come out?
Mr Tomlinson in clipped military tones. 'By the
Horseshoe Tower. Near Gatehouse. Main entrance to
castle'.

Sydney Thomson - Jones: ' We'll walk up the road round
there and pick up the Bharunians as they come out. If they
have the package - we jump them'.
Tomlinson: ' Right'. The soldiers in the party, all dressed
in civilian clothes, ready themselves. The party move
silently off up the road and round to the front of the castle.

Up ahead of the Americans and the Bharunians are nearing
the end of the tunnel. Ahead is a large rusty looking iron
grill set hard into the end of the tunnel. Sulu Wasei tells
one of his people to remove the grill. Rats scurry over his
feet. They are ignored. Loads of rats in Oshasha.
Sulu Wasei: ' Quickly'. Just then there is an ominous
rumbling noise. The tunnel collapsing behind them? –
'Get moving!'.
Sulu Wasei: ' Quickly or we're trapped!'. The party needs
no second bidding. Shoulders heave against the grill. It
won't budge. The rumbling gets louder. It sounds like
water. It's in one of the side tunnels and getting nearer.
Sulu Wasei realising at last: ' The tunnel must be a sewer
pipe for the rain!'.
Desperately the party heave against the grill. Slowly it
gives. Behind them the footsteps have increased and are

pounding round the bend in the tunnel. The approaching American party have also heard the noise but are still shielded from the Bharunians by the tunnels curve; but not for long.

Lee Elroy - Meyers:' Run! Water coming down the tunnel'. An avalanche is coming in a big wave. Like its been accumulating behind some boulders over a very long time. Now the boulders had given way.   'We'll drown!'.

Meanwhile the Bharunians, after much banging with rocks and knives and have succeeded in shifting the grill. They swarm up the ladder to another grill high above them. The moon shines down bathing everybody in a eerie light. Some of the Bharunians are crossing themselves. The upper grill, resting on grass, is quickly shoved aside, and it's everybody for themselves.
Sulu Wasei: 'Get out. Out We haven't much time'. He waves urgently to the rest of the party. They need no second bidding.
Fifty feet back down the tunnel the American party in full flight towards the ladder. The sewage and rain water which has built up behind a collapsed wall in one of the side tunnels is pouring towards them and making a great thunderous noise. ' How much further!?'. Meyers chest is hurting, his heart pumping, and the pain of it all shows on his face.
All the Americans are now running for dear life - they reach the end of the tunnel and start charging up the ladder and trying move the first grill which has been

jammed back in with stones thrown on top by the Bharunians. Several of the party are pushing and shoving upwards to get the grill open. With seconds to go the grill gives way. It's thrown aside and the group scramble up through and to the steel ladder which is embedded in the wall leading up to the second grill opening. The last two members of the team almost being washed away with the water that swirls around the lowest rungs of the ladder . Lee Elroy - Meyers - is the first through and standing on the tussocky grass. All caution thrown to the wind pulls his gun from a shoulder holster and urges everybody on. Feet scrambling up the ladder and out through the entrance. All pretense of a stealthy approach gone.

Outside and further away the Bharunians huddle together behind rocks trying to shelter against the wind, and also the rain that is lashing down. They are not far from the Horseshoe Tower; very near to the main gate of Corfe Castle. Above them looms the gaunt remains of the Tower itself, where once medieval knights would stand guard against the forces of evil from the surrounding counties of England in the middle ages. A thunder clap and then silence. Time passes, then out of this silence comes a stealthier sound of animal movement. A human body of some kind slithering with great cunning towards the Bharunian contingent. A black outline against a blacker sky and barely a quarter moon to show everything. The son et lumiere lighting display of the castle that had bathed everybody in an eerie light, controlled by timers, has now switched off. Plunging the castle into even greater darkness.   Sulu Wasei readies himself for an attack and prods the two nearest to him to stay alert. The leading soldier from the American contingent creeping stealthily through the rocks of the lower slope of the castle earthworks searching for the Bharunians. The black moon showing even less than the quarter moon it was twenty minutes ago.

Speaking into a TAC mike located at his neck the American, equipped with night x ray vision from a helmet delivering a head up display of the scene in front of him - whispers instructions back via his throat mike.

Other men from the American party start to pan out on either side, including Lee Elroy - Meyers with gun drawn. The rest have night sticks.

Another flash of lightning throws both sides into sharp relief, and in that instance we see Sulu Wasei running for dear life down the grass slope and back towards the cars. Lee Elroy - Meyers comes out of this frozen moment of time and sees Sulu Wasei running for dear life. With a sharp order to 'Move it you guys! He runs down the slope towards the car park. But he is too late this time. The Bharunians are gone. While Meyers had been looking around the Bharunians had made their way between the ancient boulders and back down the slope. Sulu Wasei had been acting as back marker to make sure the rest of the embassy staff had gone to there cars before running himself to his own vehicle. Drawing attention to himself but cutting their losses for another day.

The Americans make a detailed search around the tunnel entrance but find nothing. They talk constantly to each other on TAC phones even though they are only a few feet apart.
Lee Elroy - Meyers: ' Look. More people coming out the castle grounds.   Hiding behind those ruins...
Technical Sergeant Johnson: 'Do we get them?'.
Lee Elroy - Meyers: ' Wait for them to speak'.
An English voice whispering to the others.
 Meyers: ' It's only the us the British. Meyers hears this but does not respond. 'Come on - back to the hotel'.
The American party creep back round and away from the entrance into the gloom. Heading as fast as they can for there own transport parked down the twisting road below the castle ruins.   No one suggests talking to the Brits.
So much for international co-operation.

Tunnel Exit:

Sydney Thomson - Jones: ' Looks like nobody found the device - I need to talk to London'. He goes out to the car phone in the Government car parked at the bottom of the hill; telling London that nobody has found the device.

In an office in Old Admiralty Arches near Trafalgar Square:

A back view of a shadowy figure in a chair behind a large dark oak desk. Desk lamp glows. Heavy drape curtains drawn against the London traffic. In the far corner another

person in deep shadow listens. Cigar smoke curling towards the ceiling. Further down in Westminster Big Ben is chiming midnight.
Bong. Bong. Bong. Bong.....

The shadowy figure standing behind the desk holds the phone: ' We've found out that the device has an explosive charge attached to it. By our reckoning it will go off in 3 days time. Could be earlier.
– I'm sending you coded instructions to diffuse the charge. Members of the army disposal squad are coming directly. Give the instructions to them. Meet at your location in Swanage.

In Dorset Sydney Thomson - Jones puts the phone down.

In the early hours of the morning an Army bomb disposal van arrives and several men dressed in black get out, heading quickly for the rear of the building. Each carries a holdall. Watched with interest by some of the more elderly guests looking out of their bedrooms windows. Those who find sleep difficult.   The men go through the foyer, nodding at the night porter and on into the lift.
The night porter, an ex Royal Marine raises an eyebrow but says nothing. Lot of strange things happening this week along the coast. Especially at night....

In the bedroom at one o'clock in the morning conversation just finishing between the bomb disposal men and Sydney Thomson - Jones.

' You know as much as I we do now. You'll be part of our team until we get to the device - then it's over to you'.

The men from the Army are young, fit, competent and very no nonsense.
'We have three days Sir, at the very most, to find the device before it blows up. - a question Sir, if it's permitted?
Sydney Thomson - Jones. ' Go on I'll answer if I can'
'Do the other people looking for this device know that it's booby trapped?'. Sydney Thomson - Jones: ' I've talked to the American and South African groups who are down here, but not the French yet. The Bharunians we don't know about'.
Army Bomb Disposal officer: 'Can't very well broadcast a message to the public telling them not to touch it - they'll be panic'.
Sydney Thomson - Jones: 'I can get a message to this 'Committee for Wealth' that they have in Swingle Matravers. That's a body that organises things down here in Swingle Matravers - their person in charge of that committee is one Fred Driver.
Army: 'Who's he?'
Sydney Thomson - Jones: ' Pig farmer - big farm, very successful. Lives a mile outside the village where the tramp found it originally. Side of the road out there..'.
Army: ' And where's the tramp who found it?
Sydney Thomson - Jones: 'Nobody knows. There was a report of someone who might have been him being found

dead at the base of some cliffs. But we don't know whether it was him or not - the Bharunians might have found and questioned him, then killed him. We don't know. – Whoever <u>was</u> found at the base of the cliff the body had marks on it showing that the person had been interrogated. But we can't be certain. Not much left of somebody after they've fallen three hundred feet down a sheer cliff – onto rocks below'.

Army: ' Well, will that be all Sir? We can get some shut eye before this kicks off any further... '.

Sydney Thomson - Jones: ' For the moment. Hotel breakfast is good. Order what you want off the menu. I told them to leave sandwiches in your rooms. Two rooms with bathrooms at the end of the corridor.   Tea and coffee facilities are in there as well. Room numbers 18 and 19'.

' Good night Sir'. They leave quickly, turning to their left down the darkened corridor.

Breakfast room, following morning.

8.00 am.   The British contingent, bolstered now by the army, are having breakfast. The hotel waiter walks over to Sydney Thomson - Jones with a message. Handing over a single sheet of hotel paper. Written on the paper is a telephone number and a name. The name is Prince Okamba.

'When did this come in?'   'Just now Sir. The person did not wait. Said you should contact him'. Preparations are made. Sydney Thomson - Jones makes the call. British security personnel sit in another booth recording the telephone conversation.

Prince Okamba: ' I believe we are looking for the same thing Mr Thomson - Jones. - I am willing to do a deal with you'.

Sydney Thomson - Jones: 'Oh? What would that be?'

Prince Okamba: ' The device – in return for saving the lives of 8000 people in your seaside town of Swanage'.

Thomson - Jones: 'What exactly are you talking about?' Security personnel in the booth next door exchange looks as they hear this. The tape recorders are running, notepads on knees.

Prince Okamba: 'I am talking about a severe form of stomach ache resulting in death – from the drinking water supply'.

Thomson - Jones: 'I see' – writes frantically on a pad: " Water Board – get them here" .

Prince Okamba: 'If you are thinking of talking to anybody about this - it's too late. The poison will enter the drinking water supply in exactly one hour if we don't come to an agreement'.

Sydney Thomson - Jones keeping cool in a crises. Something he has been very good at in his career at the Foreign Office: ' I'm sure we can do that - now what exactly do you have in mind?' Looking at his watch as he says this. Out of the corner of his eye he sees several members of his team on phones.

Prince Okamba: 'One hour Mr Thomson - Jones. One hour - the stock market forecasting device to be deposited at the tourist office by 9 o'clock this morning   - in the upstairs room'.

Sydney Thomson - Jones playing for time: ' But we don't have the device - we assumed you had it'.

Prince Okamba: 'This is getting us nowhere Mr Thomson - Jones. You have until 9 o'clock'. He puts the phone down.

Sydney Thomson - Jones looks at the phone, putting it down gently. There is a soft knock on the door. It's the security personnel from the booth next door. 'We traced the call'.

' A back street bed and breakfast in Swingle Matravers?'

' Yes how did you know'. Sydney Thomson - Jones gives the security man a pitying look. 'Elementary my dear Watson. Elementary, very Elementary...'.

In the Bharunians hotel lobby in Swingle which that group had just moved into from the damp, drafty back street terraced house they had previously rented - the members of the Swingle Matravers Committee for Wealth, those that could get away from their businesses, are sunk deep in armchairs. A tray of coffee and the remains of sandwiches nearby. The party have obviously been there some time.

Fred Driver: ' Let's move'.

Bill - ' Back to Linda's place?'

Fred shakes his head.

John: 'What then?' Fred: 'We take the device to Dancing Ledge and do a deal with whomever turns up to collect it. But first we go to the tourist office on the seafront of Swanage.

Hotel Lobby:

On the wall directly behind Fred's arm chair is the end wall of the hotel lobby. On the other side in the small frontage is parked a grey laundry van with 'Smarts Laundry, Weymouth, Dorset' written on the side of it. The people inside however had nothing to do with any cleaning service. Cramped inside are the members of the British Security service all listening to the villagers conversation. They'd set up their post to listen to the Bharunians in their room, having heard they'd moved in there. The Committee for Wealth lot in the visitors coffee lounge by the main door, are an unexpected bonus.
Sydney Thomson - Jones: 'Round to the Tourist office - quickly'.
The van moves off at high speed.

A while later Fred, Bill, John and Ian all enter the tourist office on the ground floor which is full of visitors and a few of the locals. Upstairs, the tourist office had a room they rented out. In this Linda Dodswell is currently carrying out Aromatherapy sessions using her portable table and equipped with her oils and scents. Relaxation music which today consists of a celestial harp combined with the occasional hooting of whales - if the sounds drifting down the stairs are anything to go by.

On the portable massage table a large near naked female in her forties is lying covered with towels. She is receiving aromatherapy treatment, a mix of massage plus varied oils and lotions rubbed in. These are being expertly applied by Linda resplendent in her dark blue looking nurses uniform.

Linda is in the middle of one of her routines: Head, shoulders and back. Then down the legs ending with reflexology foot treatment. If time, then ten minutes of Reiki healing to finish. A one hour treatment , of which there are a further five people booked in for that day. It is 10 o'clock.

Linda is just turning the client over and attending to the head, top and front of the shoulders with Lavender Cedar and Jasmine oils wafting up from her steadily working oiled fingers. If that wasn't enough there is a lavender incense stick burning in the corner. Outside through the small skylight window kept open for ventilation, can be heard the distant sounds of the sea, and the people on swanage beach. Into this calming atmosphere comes a knock at the door.

Fred Driver in a very low voice: ' It's us Linda'.   Linda replies and prepares to slip out of the door temporarily whilst her client lies dreamily listening to whales hooting combined with the celestial harp. Drifting off to sleep...

Linda brushing her hair back with one hand in a small mirror on the wall and pulling her shirt into place where it had got rucked up with all the stretching of arms over the patients body. She quickly moves the few paces to the door reaching for the door knob.   Suddenly all hell breaks loose in the corridor outside. Pounding feet on the stairs and Fred, John and the others are violently pushed to one side as a gang of heavies barge in.   The effect is catastrophic for the Aromatherapy session.

Screaming from the rudely awakened woman on the couch. Clutching a thin towel around her barely covering her large proportions. Linda gets knocked to one side, while the cd player is stuck on the whale hooting with the volume knocked up by a security man built like a rugby prop barging straight into the coach which the screaming woman is trying to get off whilst clutching her many and varied towels. Tissues, skin scrubbers, sandalwood, jasmine, and cedar vapour oils, plus a cash box with loose change cascading over the floor. Security people everywhere towering over the two women as they search around for the brown paper parcel or whatever else might look as though it is housing the stock market device. Ripping apart the massage table with a knife, and the flimsy storage cupboards used by the tourist office for all their spare brochures, leaflets and tourist stuff sold to promote the town. Papers, office equipment and all manner of stores fly all over the place. Lee Elroy - Meyers shouting his head off over everybody. The room is now a complete wreck.

Pounding feet on the stairs and the Bharunians now charge in. Security personnel from France, America and South Africa don't like the Bharunians coming in. Try to keep them out by shutting the door. The Bharunians fight back, the small room is a melee of flying fists, people trying to strong arm each other. In the midst of the confusion Fred Driver works his way down the side of the tiny room and opens a door. Seen by several of the security types, he conspicuously throws a large brown paper package out of the window.

Down below Ian Samways from the garage retrieves the paper bag package from the back of the pickup where it has landed.

In full view of everyone including the security mob upstairs now leaning out the window he puts it in the cab. He drives off hell for leather down the road in his pickup. Wheels screeching.   The crowds in Swanage are amazed by such goings on. A small seaside resort, with heritage steam railway, beach, promenade and old fashioned tourist office. Now all these people are storming the buildings! Is it a film? Is it something to do with the millennium bug (year 2000) that is supposed to bother computer systems that everybody was warning about before Christmas? Not several months later surely?
Now all these security people seem to be storming out of the front of the tourist building and heading off in their cars and vans back down the promenade where hundreds of people are on the beach. Heads turning to see what is going on. Cars and vans streaming north out of Swanage along the promenade road.   Is it a film ? Where's the film crew?! What's the title? Who's in it? Anybody famous? Few of the residents had seen anything like it.

The convoy of cars disappear round the bend at the end of the town towards Studland.   Upstairs in the Tourist information office, Linda, John and Bill look at each other in silence. The woman on the table, who was not part of anything, has long gone - shouting that she would be making a complaint against the police and anybody else she could think of. They start to clear up the mess. Putting everything back where it came from. Righting the furniture and taking down the massage table. What's left of it.   Linda not likely to be invited back to the tourist office again! Some 8 minutes go by. Fred looks at his watch and moves to a small safe hidden behind one of the stationery cupboards. Unlocks it and produces the real package containing the device.

'Dancing Ledge?' Says Linda. 'Dancing Ledge' the others chorus. We'll see who makes the highest bid. They troop downstairs past the bemused tourist office staff where Linda smiles demurely and hands over the key to the upstairs room. The public looking at brochures about the Waverley Paddle steamer coming into the pier for it's customary trips to Weymouth, the Isle of Wight and Bournemouth. Moving quickly over to Fred's Land Rover and dumping Linda's table and bags of ointments and lotions into the back of it. The Committee for Wealth start on the final leg of this, there latest adventure and by no means their last adventure.

The Pig Farm:

Meanwhile Ian is leading the Americans, the French, the South Africans a merry dance through the Dorset countryside as he decoys the security people away from the rest of the Committee and heads for the Pig Farm. Bodies and security equipment are being flung around everywhere as cars and vans screech round quiet Dorset roads.. Several times Ian has diverted off roads and gone down dirt tracks and bridal paths deeper and ever deeper in the Purbeck countryside. Heading more away from Fred Driver's pig farm than towards it. But eventually he turns and heads in that direction. Back towards Corfe Castle and Swingle Matravers.

Meanwhile, oblivious to all this, Jane Driver in one of the barns near to the entrance is trying to deliver piglets from one of the large sows they have on the farm; otherwise known as Large White.
Jane, Fred's wife has been working at it for hours moving between one row of sows after another checking the piglets that have come and looking for potential problems. There are nearly a hundred sows in the large byre and with the farm hands they have been at the delivery of the new born seemingly for ever. This particular sow though will not yield up her piglets and there are clearly problems requiring the use of a vet. Like all farmers she has one eye on vets bills so has delayed calling for the vet until it is absolutely necessary. When she did do she found that he was over the other side of the county dealing with a horse.

Jane had not been aware that he dealt with horses particularly. His not being an equestrian veterinary practice. Either way he'd said that he would be on his way shortly, his partner a young woman recently joined from Veterinary College was in bed with flu. So she was rather surprised to hear in the distance the sound of a helicopter and cars approaching. Fred has not had time to warn Jane of what is happening.

In the chase several of the cars have been gaining on Ian, his twisting and turning around Dorset lanes through the hamlets and small villages in the area had not thrown them off. The chase cars however had not had it all there own way. One car had spun on mud left by a farm tractor and had gone crashing straight through a gate entrance. Coming to a halt up to it's axles in thick mud.

Another had ended up in a ditch with it's tyre blown out. The police helicopter had not helped. Coming very low over the chase cars in order to distract the driver of the pick up truck. Unfortunately he had also distracted young Christopher Little who at the age of 19 and who not yet taken his basic police driving course. His police driving experience being limited to a nervous journey driving the local police inspector and a female social worker to a village in order to discuss what several local women had been repeatedly doing out on the streets in the small hours of the morning.

Christopher had had virtually no contact with the two police cars at his station apart from washing them. His driving experience at home being to get behind the wheel

of his Fathers 1960s Vauxhall Victor 101 FC Estate car
which had been restored at enormous expense (complete
rip off as far as Chris was concerned) by that out and out
charlatan, Ian Samways, at the garage in Swingle.
Now there was this caper, charging around the countryside
with helicopters flying about. He had gained more
experience of police driving in the past hour on what his
father had called 'real roads', than he had had in the past
year behind the wheel of his fathers classic car. He was
now driving in convoy at speed with a lot of het up people
all yelling at him to put his foot down and keep up with the
cars in front!

Driving, as he was, now, through dark country lanes
Christopher had thought he'd got the hang of this driving
lark when suddenly a black shape of the helicopter
looming up out of the sky and flying very low over the
hedgerows straight at him. Christopher had crashed the
car into the back of the one in front and had promptly been
pranged by a big police van coming up behind. They had
all had to bundle into the back of one of the police vans.

Jane meanwhile had come out into the farmyard, thinking
that the vet had gone over the top in his response to her
phone call for dealing with the delivery of one pig.
Standing staring at all the cars crowding into the courtyard.
Not to mention the helicopter people, still hidden, that now
appeared to be shouting through a megaphone for
everybody to stay calm and not move! Really, Jane

thought, she really MUST have a word with the vet! How much was he charging for all this lot she'd like to know! She'd known the roads we're congested at this time of year but *surely* he had not required all this police support to help him get to their farm!   To her surprise she sees her husband jump out of one vehicle and hand a parcel to Ian, who has abandoned the pick up truck in the middle of the yard and is now on a scrambler motorbike. He revs up and with a scream of wheels heads hell for leather out the opposite end of the farmyard leaving the police standing there. Haring off across the fields at the back. Making for the coast road to Swanage and as the police and rest of them we're to find out later, to Dancing Ledge several miles away.

The occupants of the cars see the handover (as is intended), and the bike with its earth shattering roar. The bike disappearing round the back of the milking sheds and out of another exit at the back of the farm complex. The chase is on again as people who had got out of their vehicles at the run now reverse their actions and throw themselves back in the various cars and vans. Charging towards and all trying to get out at once through the restricted farm entrance.

Fred and Jane Driver watch them go. When the last vehicle has disappeared up the lane Fred walks slowly back to his Land Rover, moves a blanket back. On the backseat and under the blanket is the real device. The package handed to young Ian Samways was another decoy. Fred Driver covers it up again and he and his wife head back to the farmhouse just as the vet arrives in his car to deal with pig. Of the Bharunians, there is no sign.

CHAPTER ELEVEN.
THE BHARUNIANS

While all this had been going on the Bharunian contingency are in their hotel room listening to Sulu Wasei with Prince Okamba observing. All eyes are on Sulu Wasei who is trying to persuade Prince Okamba: as to the next move in this hopeless saga of trying to compete with four major security services trying to obtain the stock market forecasting device. Prince Okamba is counting off a tally on his fingers.
Prince Okamba: 'So far you have suggested that we:
1) Search the village - Nothing.
2) Go down a sewer pipe leading to the castle.
Sulu Wasei interrupts: 'But that was an ancient tunnel that was supposed to lead to a strong room of the ruined castle'. Prince Okamba waves dismissively and continues.
3) That we should stalk the other groups all round the village. Which we did without success.
4) That we raid the Aromatherapy clinic (!?) Interrupting the session between the Therapist and her middle aged lady client on the table - to try and track down the device there.
Sulu Wasei tries to interrupt again but Prince Okamba waves him down..

–- only to find that we have been beaten to it by all the other people who are looking for that device as well. Also all we get for our pains is the sight of the woman running half naked out the back of the clinic via the emergency fire exit.

Some members of the group have a flashback pictures of the now hysterical woman on the couch now running out of the emergency exit door above the tourist office. The security people charging back down the narrow stairs to the ground floor and out the front entrance.

Prince Okamba, bringing everybody back to the hotel room: 'So you think we should go out to the farm of this Mr Driver and try and find the device there? – you think this will save your neck? The Bharunians do not know that the other countries including the British have just been out there and found nothing. Or about the wild goose chase they are being led on across the countryside by Ian Samways on his mountain bike.

Sulu Wasei: 'It's the only logical place left'.

Prince Okamba with heavy irony: 'I would not have thought that logic has helped you so far in the search'.

The hotel rooms phone rings. Prince Okamba answers it. He listens politely, says a few words of acknowledgment and then puts the phone down. Turning to Sulu Wasei and knowing that the rest of the group are listening.

Prince Okamba 'Your logic has not worked Sulu Wasei. That was Mr Driver ringing on behalf of the Swingle Matravers 'Committee for Wealth' ... They wish to meet on the coast.

Sulu Wasei just stands and stares at Prince Okamba.

Prince Okamba: 'They want to trade. You know what that is Sulu Wasei? You can guess what they have to trade? Sulu Wasei hangs his head.

Prince Okamba: You guessed it. The device. They want £2 Million pounds for it. Raising his voice. 'Two million pounds'. This for the benefit of the rest of the group.

Sulu Wasei: ' We do not have that money. Do we?'

Prince Okamba: ' In our Embassy bank account we do. I don't think they will be satisfied with whatever we can get out of a bank cash machine with our cards.

Sulu Wasei: ' We steal it from them?'

Prince Okamba looks at the expression of sheer hopeless despair on Sulu Wasei's face. This 'Head of Intelligence' that has proved to be such a disappointment.

Prince Okamba: ' Yes. Sulu Wasei we steal it from them. Have you any other suggestions?

Sulu Wasei: ' Where?'

Prince Okamba: 'Dancing Ledge' – along the coast - about 4 miles from Swanage. - at Midnight. On Mr Drivers timing we have twenty minutes to prepare and about another twenty to get out there. We also have to avoid anybody else if we want to make a deal....... So prepare..!

Meanwhile Ian Samways is on his motorbike weaving and dashing around the countryside. The helicopter, police units, cars and vans of the security service are trying in vain to follow Ian as he goes first across fields, then pathways, then tracks and then roads and back to fields. They are at the Purbeck stone quarries at the back of Worth Matravers.   Ian, who is a very keen off road enthusiast where bikes are concerned, is enjoying himself judging by the expression on his face.

In clear view of the chasing cars and pinned in the helicopters searchlights Ian pulls out of a pannier bag on the side of the motorbike a large package in a bright white coloured bag. Caught by the lights from the helicopter now hovering overhead he flings it high over the boundary wall to the quarry and rides on, back wheel spinning and sliding over before regaining traction. Stones and mud spitting up off the ground as he scrambles past. The chase cars and van charge headlong down a stony quarry road after the package. Lights coming on in the works cottages further on. People standing at the doors and upstairs bedroom windows. Torches being flashed about. Shouted comments to other neighbours as to what the heck is going on...etc etc.

Big action sequence as the chopper dramatically hovers overhead. The twin searchlights slung underneath providing the only light down onto the black stygian gloom of the quarry. No street lighting up here at the back of Worth Matravers. Certainly not on the quarry roads. Mad scramble between the security forces to get to the device first. Headlights from a circle of cars illuminate the scene - the helicopter looming overhead. It's searchlight glares down. Car and van doors slamming. People running. The head of the French contingent gets to the package first. Others hard on his heels and panting over his shoulder at what the man has in his hands. Turning and running for cover expecting it to be booby trapped. A shout to the Frenchman to put it on the ground and run for it.   Bomb disposal experts stepping forward hastily dressed in their protection. Opening it very cautiously.   Staring with disbelief at the contents.

A teddy bear grins back at them. A cuddly Father Christmas toy with a red battery light attached to its head. The light winks on and off and a notice pinned to the front says: ' Fooled You!'. The Frenchman steps up behind the military personnel, rips off the notice and stares at it. Other people gathering round to assess it and looking at each other in frustration.

CHAPTER TWELVE.
DANCING LEDGE.   MIDNIGHT.

It is ten minutes to midnight. The Bharunians are in position hiding behind rocks to one side of Dancing Ledge. The sea pounds on the lower part of the ledge into a cauldron of spray and fume 30 to 40 feet away. Not a place to be in almost pitch darkness. Clouds in thin tendrils etched across a sliver of moon.

Prince Okamba: ' Get your men ready Sulu Wasei . Your last chance remember. Your last chance. – think of the post in the market square in Oshasha - it will spur you on.

Dancing Ledge at the level of the roadway up above shows other cars arriving. People getting out and making their way across to the footpath leading to the ledge. Very stealthy. Very quiet. An air of tension. Everybody is waiting. The helicopter, which had been hovering above Fred Drivers farmhouse and had followed the security people to the Ledge has retreated. But can be heard further off. Only the people on the ground can make out whatever is going to happen, happen.

Meanwhile down on the ledge itself: Prince Okamba: 'Well Sulu Wasei?' The people from the village are over there'. He points with his ornate stick to a series of high jagged rocks that loom up over to the side of the darkened ledge itself. High tide and the sea pounding in. The Phoebe is still there but now leaning almost horizontal. The sea pounding over the Bridge and Forecastle of the ship. The ships black rusted barnacled hull rearing up in the moonlight. The sea massive and thunderous in the darkness of the rocky ledges just beyond the ship. The rough wood and stone stairway set into the cliff side leading up to safety of the cliff path seems a long way away. The Bharunians feel exposed standing near the middle of all this mayhem. They should really have remained over by the steps. Or preferably up on the cliff! Not standing exposed near the middle of the ledge with the ship looming over them and making groaning noises as it leans first one way then another. Its keel stuck in a crevice of the rock.

Dancing Ledge is not immune to rock falls either. Notices abound everywhere up on the pathways and even at the top of the stairway leading down. The Phoebe itself is acting as a breakwater against some of the rougher seas that are shipping in to the ledge. But not nearly enough for anybody to feel safe. The sea lapping ever further over the raised section of the ledge where they are huddled.

Sulu Wasei gets up and starts his walk towards the villagers. Keeping away from the seaward side.   He is flanked by two others. They are acting as bodyguards - wary - alert for anything that will happen. Sulu Wasei carries a briefcase containing the ransom, or as much as they have been able to get hold of.
The Swingle Matravers contingent led by Fred Driver, get up from behind the rocks . The foreign party are coming towards them. Fred and company move out to the centre ground. . The rain starts to come down. The roaring sound of the sea. Dark and menacing.
Sulu Wasei tries to speak as he approaches Fred Driver who by now seems to be standing near the very edge of the ledge itself. The sea pounding in only a few feet below him. Sulu's words are drowned by the noise of the sea, the wind and the rain, drumming down onto the ledge itself.

Fred Driver - yelling to make himself heard - ' You have the money!?'.
Sulu Wasei eyes him with caution. Wasei tries to speak as he approaches Fred who is by now standing near the edge of the ledge itself. The heart pounding rhythmic throbbing of the sea as it beats against the lower part of the ledge. Sulu Wasei's reply is drowned by the noise.

Fred repeats his request about the money. Sulu indicates
he does have the money and Fred insists on seeing it. '
Show me then. No tricks mind'. They move back a
considerable distance towards a cleft in the rocks. Fred's
party switching on all their torches and bringing the light
to bear on the briefcase as Sulu kneels down on the wet
ground behind the cleft and fumbles with the locks on the
case.

Above on the cliffs matters are coming to a head in more
ways than one.
Lee Elroy - Meyers trying to shelter with his team from the
driving rain. Further over they are shadowed by British
security. Meyers screams at his team. ' What are you
waiting for? Fred Driver's got it. ......Get him!!'

The Americans scramble down the rock strewn steps,
which are wet with rain and spray. Some slip and fall but
others make it. The rest of the groups follow the American
example. Except for the British contingent who remain
above, watching. The tall thin figure of Sydney Thomson -
Jones, standing sentinel against the madness that is going
on below.
The waves crash onto the rocks. It pours down in torrents.
We move to Fred Driver and Sulu Wasei as they start to
make a handover of what there is to be had. Taking the
briefcase. Fred Driver making it clear to Sulu Wasei that
its not enough. Bundles of British Bank notes tied together.
Below on the rocks the Americans are still trying to get to
the part of the ledge where the two are standing. The

wind, rain, and sea are swirling around. Constant thunder of the sea on the outer rocks.

High above looking down upon the ledge are the British, as the Americans move single file over the rocks towards the handover going on. The bag containing the device is eventually handed over to Sulu Wasei. The handover is going ahead though Fred is clearly not happy and is waving his arms about.

Suddenly out of nowhere a gigantic wave, powerful, awe inspiring, whipped up far out to sea, engulfing the Phoebe, picking it up as though it we're made of wood and slamming it back down on the ledge. Dancing Ledge seems to tremble as it takes the fall weight of the ship slamming back down. The handover has just been completed as the wave hits. Fred Driver and the others have got the brief case and other bags of money. Fred glimpses what looks like a mini tsunami out of the corner of his eye and shouts a warning. 'Run...!!'. Sulu Wasei turns to see the wave. Stands - terrified with the device in his hands. The wave crashes down on the upper ledge.

From above we look down and see Fred Driver running for his life with his companions. Making it safely, just, to the iron ladder at the side of the ledge and clinging on with the briefcase. The others carrying the further bags of money that had been produced after Fred had complained that the briefcase load was not enough to effect the hand over. A rope being tied around him by another member of the village 'Committee for Wealth' . The committee members starting to scramble up the rocks and the iron ladder and the other rocky steps leading up to safety, helped by some of the British military who are above them.

Meanwhile Sulu Wasei is standing transfixed watching the oncoming torrent of waves threatening to engulf the whole ledge. The others shout at him to run but he is memorized by the terrible power of the wave. He struggles to maintain his grip and attempts to fling the package containing the device to Prince Okamba a few feet away who is shouting at him to run. Okamba tries and fails to catch it. Sulu Wasei is caught by the wave but manages to cling on to an iron stanchion driven into the rocks.

An underwater scene of the wave and peoples legs and bodies as they cling on for all there lives are worth.

Gradually the wave recedes and we see the device floating away out of reach. Completely out of reach.

Prince Okamba stares at the device just as it sinks beneath the waves, its red and blue lights still winking on and off. An underwater view as the device sinks away and out of sight.

On the face of Prince Okamba there is a stricken look of failure, knowing that his life is probably also forfeit.

Up above, Fred Driver stands with the briefcase and money bags. Only Sydney Thomson - Jones remains standing looking out to sea. He turns to Fred Driver.
' You won Mr Driver. You won. More money for the poor of the your village?'
Fred Driver. 'Yes but nowhere near what we thought!'.
Thomson - Jones smiles bleakly at Fred. Inwardly disappointed that they did not get the device for the Government after all. Turns away, walking back to his waiting car. A tall erect figure dressed in a dark suit.

Fred stares after him – realizing that maybe his mission to help the rural poor is the right one. That after all his and the efforts of the members of the 'Committee for Wealth' are worth it. He walks off with the brief case stuffed full of notes. The others carrying the rest of the money bags. Heading for where the Land Rover is parked. By no means the two million pounds that he was looking for, but enough to repair the proverbial church roof and the scout hut, if they got some poor mutt to do it for them voluntary..

Prince Okamba and Sulu Wasei are led away to claim political asylum. About the only way they will both avoid the execution post in the middle of the town square of Oshasha. The rest of the Embassy staff follow suit

And what happened to Harry the Tramp?

On a beach in Barbados a man in over loud beach wear is sprawled across a deck chair, surrounded by young ladies. A craggy hairy man more used to the roads and streets of his native Dorset raises a glass, smiles, and says:

To the 'Committee for Wealth' . Long may they rule....!

Dorset's gentleman of the road - has come a long way since he picked up the secret device and got paid a handsome gratuity of a thousand pounds by Fred Driver and his Committee, plus a First class return plane ticket to Barbados - for a six week package holiday. With a labouring job on Fred Drivers farm at the end of it all and a rented room at the farm for as long as he wants it. Just part of the deal making that went on with the 'Committee for Wealth' – that they are all so good at.

Postscript.

If you have enjoyed reading both Lottery Mania and Dancing Ledge then do not worry - the Swingle Matravers 'Committee for Wealth' will ride again in:
Midnight on the 18th Hole.

See below for the first part of the first Chapter in this new story .   Long may they reign......!

MIDNIGHT on the 18TH HOLE.

By Brian George

 A Comedy Drama with many twists and turns to keep you enthralled. Family Reading.

Preamble and authors notes:

Midnight on the 18th Hole is the 3rd book in the trilogy written about the villagers of Swingle Matravers, Dorset and their attempts to garner money and good fortune to benefit the villagers in every way they can think of. The villagers operate the 'Committee for Wealth' as the controlling body for these nefarious borderline legal activities.

The first two books: LOTTERY MANIA and DANCING LEDGE
are fully available on Amazon, Apple Book, Kobo, Barnes and
Noble, Scribd.

Midnight on the 18th Hole was written in 2002 by the author and is
based on the town and the actual ruined abbey at Melrose in the
Border Reivers area of Scotland.

Introduction to Midnight on the 18th Hole:

Historically the Border Reivers we're raiders made up of both
English and Scottish people. They raided the border towns and
countryside between England and Scotland in between the 13th and
the 17th Centuries. Just about describes the attitude of Swingle
Matravers, Dorset, when it comes to getting money out of people!

The story starts with the local drunk named Angus who thinks he has
just seen a lot of ghostly cowled monks walking and chanting in
procession during a foggy night in the ruined grounds of Melrose
Abbey. Mainly seen out the bottom of a bottle the local district nurse
is thinking. The drunk Angus stumbles into the local police station
to tell the police sergeant all about it...!

CHAPTER ONE.
THE DRUNK.

Old drunk Angus Mc Loughlin staggers down the road late at night
alongside the River Tweed,. The road and river pass close to the
ancient ruins of Melrose Abbey. The area is bleak, with high hills in
the background.

As he moves along Angus mutters about his long ago divorced wife.
He stops, looks around and begins to sing; waving his empty beer
bottle around as he does so.
'Show me the way to go home. I'm tired and I wanno go to bed...'
He suddenly halts his singing and stares, agog, at the Abbey.

Angus: What.....who are they!???'

In the deserted ruins of the Abbey where no man or woman sensibly
walks in the early hours can be seen, through the darkness and dank
mist chilling the bone can be a long line of monks in their cowled
habits. They move silently down the ruin's nave toward the former
pulpit area.

The drunk Angus does a double -take, is puzzled at the sight and
frightened as eerie skin crawling high music rises from the abbey.

Angus plucking up some Dutch courage from the bottle: Right then!
He stumbles towards the granite wall that surrounds the ruins.
As he nears the abbey, a large, stout woman in a nightdress appears
at a window across the road, snorts at Angus' noise and slams her
window shut.

Angus throws her a middle finger and turns again to the abbey.

Angus: 'I'm going to bloody well find out what's going on, if it's the
last thing I do' . It very nearly is as he trips over a stone and falls flat
on his face in the grass. He gropes his way to the wall and pulls
himself up high enough to look over and see the line of monks still
moving solemnly down the nave.

The monks carry either gold or silver candlesticks as they approach
the remains of the alter where a beautiful nearly naked, teenage
blond girl is tied to a slab.

Angus: 'Christ! So the stories are true. There is a pagan ritual goin'
on'.
Angus continues to stare at the blond girl as the monks cluster
around her. The atmosphere is ghostly and the wind begins to rise.
Eerie music comes from somewhere and rises toa crescendo.

John Mc Tavitt's face partially obscured by his cowl stands over the
girl with a large curved scimitar held high. In a flash the sword
comes down. The moon appearing from behind a cloud suddenly
lighting up the scene. There is a blood curdling scream from the girl
on the slab. Angus also screams and falls arse over elbow onto the
rocky ground behind him.

Melrose police station. Midnight.

An old room with a blazing log fire in the grate and Sergeant
Hammond is well into his night shift. He is also well into his
whiskey as the bottle nearby on the desk is half empty. He is elderly,
nearing retirement for the second time. Thin in face and body and in
bad humour.

A fire burns in the grate, recently banked up by his assistant, a young
constable fresh out of training and finding out what it was like at a
provincial police station. An ancient clock ticks on the mantelpiece.
Another, a Tallboy grandfather clock does the same in the far corner
of this dowdy room painted in brown and cream with furniture to
match. Most of it old and scratched, like the sergeant himself if the
truth be known.

The sergeant, not liking his routine being disturbed is listening to yet
another one of Angus Mc Loughlin's stories about the Abbey. The
expression on his face tells us that the good Sergeant has heard it all

before and he does not believe a word about ghosts, the evil eye, or naked girls on slabs.

'Well Angus you a talks a good story. Mind you did that when we we're at school together - always top of the class for story telling, especially when you we're late. What that teacher of ours had to put with from you well...' Sergeant Hammond sighed.
'What! Anybody would think I'd made it up!'
Angus is very "hot under the collar" about it all. Sergeant Hammond sighs and again and looks at the clock. 'Did cross my mind Angus'
Angus looks affronted ' what'd you take me for?!'

Alright, so what *do* you want me to do ? Go over to the Abbey and see for myself? Go out there at midnight and take a look around in all this freezing fog! Meet every drunk in Melrose - meaning glance at Angus - coming back from the pub late?
Angus McLaughlin standing, or trying to stand on his dignity as a man of the road 'Yes that's exactly what I want you to do'. Hastily adding: 'No sense in me going over there on my own'.

The door swings open and Midwife Mrs Rose Scott hurries in. She ignores Angus with a sniff and addresses the sergeant.
Rose is 45 years old, smartly dressed in a dark blue midwife's uniform and has a very brisk, some people would say caustic, no nonsense manner when it suits her. Which is most of the time as far as her young patients we're concerned. She does not suffer fools. Though can be surprisingly gentle when faced with a genuine case of distress.

Sergeant Hammond assuming his official pose: 'How are things Rose?'

Rose Scott bustling about and making a business of sitting and looking pointedly at the electric kettle on the side before speaking: 'Delivered young Helen Thompson of twins this evening. Ouch.

She'll be in the cottage hospital for a while I'm thinking.
Complications. Needs the rest in hospital. Bad weather as well'.
Looking out the window and wondering if anybody is going to take
the hint and put the kettle on. The sergeant signs to a young
constable to make some tea.

Rose continuing: - Blowing up a blizzard I'm thinking.
Sergeant: 'Aye, right enough. Turning to Angus .. You'll be wanting
to hear what Angus has seen down at the Abbey'.
Rose turns a disgusted look on old Angus. They are of a similar age
although Angus looks much older due to his drinking and poor
lifestyle.
'And what's the old sot been seeing from the end of his bottle this
time? Fairies is it? Or ghosties again?

Angus very indignant: ' As a matter of fact it was monks I saw...' He
got no further.. 'Monks is it? Ghosts I suppose? Said Rose jumping
in, she had no respect for Angus and had heard it a dozen times
before.

Angus ignoring this rude remark: 'About half an hour ago'.

Rose more softly now: ' That's funny, thought I saw someone in a
monks habit as I cycled up the road. Ach! never heard such
nonsense!'

For more of the story - lookout for publication of:
Midnight on the 18th Hole!
(Being worked on right now - 27th March 2019.
Nottingham. UK

Blank page

Blank page

Blank page

Blank page

Blank page

Blank page